This book belongs to:

_____

A gift from:

_____

THE BIG BOOK FOR
TODDLERS

edited by Alice Wong
& Lena Tabori

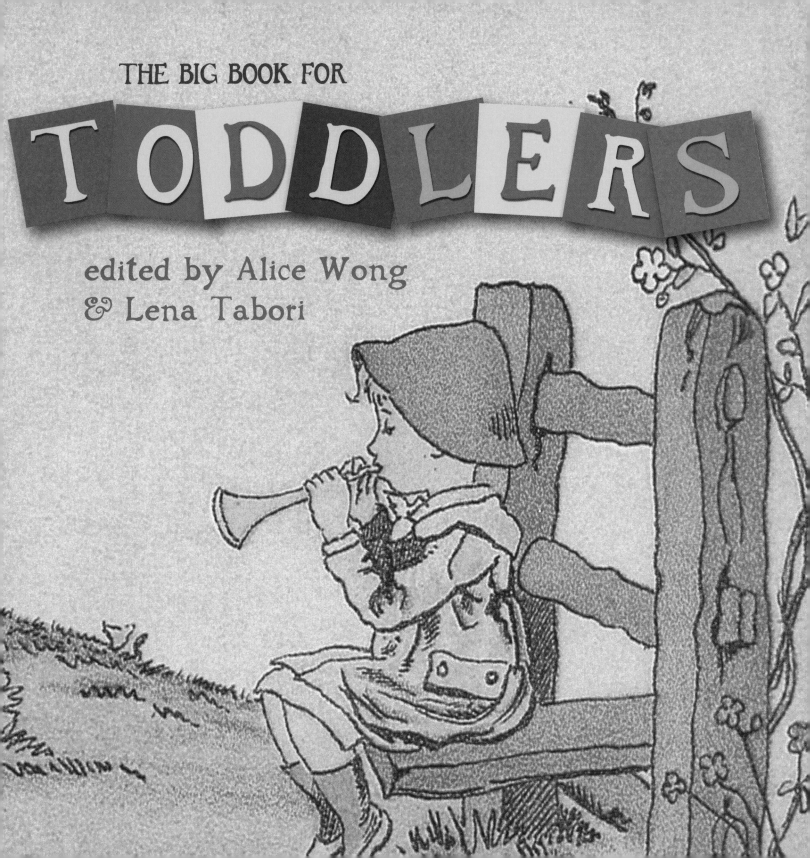

Published in 2009 by Welcome Books®
An imprint of Welcome Enterprises, Inc.
6 West 18th Street
New York, NY 10011
www.welcomebooks.com

Text by Sara Baysinger, Katrina Fried, Deirdra Garcia, Nicholas Liu, Jacinta O'Halloran,
Monique Peterson, Wendy Wax, Alice Wong
Musical arrangements by Frank Zuback
Line Illustrations by Megan Halsey, Sarah Kaplan, Kathryn Shaw
Designed by Amanda Webster and Kristen Sasamoto

Art Credits:
Front & back cover art by Jessie Willcox Smith; Pgs. 5, 99: Hilda Austin; Pg. 12: Dovis M. Ward; Pg. 20: Lawson
Wood; Pg. 39: Margaret Evans Price; Tiny Boats J.H. Hartley; Pg 45: The P. & M. Company, Inc.; Pg. 46: Kate
Greenaway; Pgs. 50, 82: Maxfield Parrish; Pgs. 60-61, 68: Eul Alie; Pg. 62: Lenski; Pgs. 72-72: E. Curtis; Pgs. 74-75:
Ida Waugh; Pg. 80: Margaret Evans Price; Pg. 83: Peter Fraser; Pg. 109: Fern Bisel Peat; Pgs. 115, 116, 145: Frank
Hart; Pg. 131 Rosa C. Petherick; Pgs. 138-139: John Gee; Pg. 155 C.M. Bird; Pgs. 198, 201: Frances Brundage; Pg,
212: R.H. Porteous

Library of Congress Cataloging-in-Publication Data on file.

ISBN: 978-1-59962-071-8

Printed in China

First Edition

10 9 8 7 6 5 4 3 2 1

CONTENTS

Activities & Crafts

◎ Nursery Rhymes

◎ Games

◉ Songs

◎Fairy Tales

Activities & Crafts

Christmas Decorations

GLITTER STARS

wax paper, glue, glitter or confetti, scissors, string

1. Draw stars with glue on a sheet of wax paper and fill in the shapes with a thin layer of glue.
2. Sprinkle glitter or confetti on the glue shapes.
3. Allow to dry; cut out stars.
4. To hang stars, pierce a small hole in the end of one point and loop a piece of string through it.

PAPER CHAIN

scissors, multicolored construction paper, markers, glitter, glue

1. Cut several 5-inch strips of paper. Try cutting zig-zaggy, squiggly, and wavy edges.
2. Decorate with markers or glitter.

3. Glue one strip closed into a ring.
4. Thread another strip into the first ring, then glue shut.
5. Continue connecting rings until the chain is as long as desired. Use as streamers or as tree decoration.

STOCKING ORNAMENT

red construction paper, scissors, tape, hole puncher, yarn, markers, glue, cotton balls

1. Cut same-sized stocking shapes from 2 pieces of paper and tape edges, except the top, together.
2. Punch a hole at the top end and loop yarn through.
3. Write name and decorate with markers.
4. Glue cotton balls around top of stocking.
5. Insert notes, pictures, sticker, or other little surprises into stocking and hang on tree.

A Circus Train

*small pantry-item boxes (such as empty tea or cracker boxes),
scissors, brown wrapping paper, tape, paintbrushes, finger paint,
markers, glue, buttons, large paper clips*

Collect small boxes as cars for bears, kangaroos, tigers, giraffes,
lions, elephants, and other circus animals. Cut brown wrapping
paper and use tape to wrap it around each box. With finger paints,
make thumb and finger prints along the sides of the boxes to
create various animal bodies. Then use a marker to draw animal
eyes, ears, tails, and feet on the thumbprint bodies. Using
paintbrushes, add bars to the circus cars and decorate the tops
and ends of each car. Glue buttons on each car to make train
wheels. To connect the cars, straighten paper clips and bend
each end to point down at a 90-degree angle. Poke holes in
the ends of each car, then insert paper clip ends into the holes
to link the cars together. Get ready to step right up and
see the big-top show!

Easter Bunny Eggs

pot, water, white eggs, spoon, wax crayons, pink egg dye,
bowl, scissors, pink paper, tape

1. Fill pot with water and boil eggs for 10 to 15 minutes, then remove with spoon and let cool.
2. Decorate eggs with wax crayons by drawing two circles for eyes, an upside-down triangle for a nose, whiskers on each side, and two front teeth.
3. Prepare dye in bowl, dip each egg into dye, and let dry.
4. Draw and cut out long ears from pink paper, then glue them on to each egg.
5. Cut a 4 x 1/2-inch strip of paper and tape ends together to form rings.
6. Set bunny eggs on rings to stand and leave for your child to discover.

Egg Carton Insects

cardboard egg cartons, scissors, tempera paint, paintbrushes, pipe cleaners, googly eyes, markers

Ant: 3 cups, 2 antennae, 6 legs; blue paint

Caterpillar: 4 to 6 cups, 2 antennae; green paint

Ladybug: 1 cup, 2 antennae, 6 legs; red and black paints

Spider: 1 cup, 8 legs; black paint

To make egg carton insects, cut one to six cups from an egg carton. Decorate with tempera paint and let dry. To make legs, poke a hole in the side of each cup and insert pipe cleaners. To make antennae, poke two small holes in the top of the first cup and insert pipe cleaners. Glue on googly eyes and draw on a mouth. Will the insects save the colony, become warriors, or just join the circus?

Galactic Mobile

Markers, cardboard, scissors, aluminum foil, hole punch, string, glue, glitter, yellow plastic container lid, four yellow or orange pipe cleaners, Styrofoam balls, paint, paintbrush, toothpicks, plastic lid, large needle, thread, two sticks about a foot long

MOON

1. Draw a crescent or full moon on cardboard. Cut out and wrap with aluminum foil.
2. Punch a hole near the top. Thread string through and attach to the mobile base.

STARS

1. Draw different-sized stars on cardboard. Make some with longer and shorter points.
2. Spread a thin layer of glue on top and sprinkle each with a different color glitter. Let dry. Repeat on other side.
3. Punch a hole near the end of a point. Thread string through and tie to mobile base.

SUN

1. Cut eight small equally spaced slits along the rim of the yellow plastic lid.
2. Bend each pipe cleaner into a V-shape, and slip the two ends into a slit. You should have the bent part sticking out to form triangular sunbeams all around the lid edge.
3. Thread a piece of string through one of the top triangles and attach to mobile base.

PLANETS

1. Create the eight planets using different-sized Styrofoam balls and paint. Design each of the planets with a different characteristic:
   * Mercury is half the size of Earth, making it the second smallest planet in the solar system. It has a gray surface.
   * Venus is about the size of Earth and has a thick cloud cover that reflects sunlight and makes it appear white.
   * Earth is medium-sized, with water and clouds on the planet's surface, making it appear blue with white swirls.
   * Mars is smaller than Earth and has a fiery red color.
   * Jupiter is the largest planet and has swirls of brown, white, gray, and blue.
   * Saturn is encircled by thin, prominent rings. Create the rings by inserting two toothpicks opposite from each other on each side of a ball. Cut out the center of a plastic lid, leaving enough room for the planet, and then slip on top of the toothpicks to create the ring.
   * Uranus is a large planet. Methane gases in the atmosphere cause it to appear blue-green.
   * Neptune contains a layer of cold water around its core that moves to the surface and becomes a gas, giving the large planet a bluish color.
2. To hang, have a grown-up thread a large needle with thread and knot it. Push the needle through the bottom of the planet so it comes out the top. The knot should catch on the bottom. Tie to the mobile.

MOBILE BASE

1. Use string to bind the two sticks together in the middle so they make an X-shape.
2. Attach a string from the center of the X so you can hang the mobile.
3. Hang your sun in the center of the mobile and then arrange planets around it in the order of their distance from the sun: Mercury, Venus, Earth, Mars, Jupiter, Saturn, Uranus, Neptune. Fill in with moon and stars!

Halloween Crafts

PIPE CLEANER SPIDERS

Black pipe cleaners, string

1. Twist pipe cleaners together to form round bodies with eight legs each.

2. Attach string and hang from door-frame to about top-of-head height. Scatter little ones around house.

FINGERPRINT SHAPES

Black inkpad, paper, markers, glue, glitter, scissors

1. Let children make as many Halloween shapes as they can come up with using fingerprints and markers. Add glowing eyes with dabs of glue and glitter. Cut out shapes to decorate house.

Some suggestions:

Spider: thumbprint; draw on legs.
Cat: pinky print for head, thumbprint for body; draw on ears, tail, and legs.
Owl: pinky print for head, thumbprint for body; draw on ears and claw feet.
Bat: thumbprint; draw on wings.

THE MUMMY GAME

Rolls of cheap toilet paper

1. Whoever is chosen to be the mummy stands with arms and legs apart.

2. Wrap up the mummy with toilet paper!

3. Mummy chases the other children (arms front, legs straight, clumps around and moans). Yikes!

TUB OF WORMS

Cooked spaghetti, oil, plastic tub, wrapped candy, several peeled whole grapes, baby carrots, blindfold (optional)

1. Prepare tub before children arrive. Mix spaghetti with a bit of oil to get things slimy. Add wrapped candy, grapes, and carrots.

2. Children feel around the "worms" to find treats. Do not pull out anything that feels like eyeballs and fingers!

Homemade Valentines

LACY DOILY VALENTINE

red construction paper, tape, glue, doily

1. Cut 2 hearts out of red paper
2. Hinge them together with tape.
3. Glue the bottom heart onto the white doily
4. Lift the top heart to write your message.

THREE-DIMENSIONAL VALENTINE

red paper, scissors, stapler

1. Cut 4 hearts out of red paper and place on top of each other.
2. Fold hearts in half vertically to crease, and staple together down the center along the crease.
3. Spread open all the sides to make a three-dimensional heart.
4. Print a message on all 16 sides of the heart.

VALENTINE PENDANT

cardboard, red paper, aluminum foil, glue, pink ribbon

1. Cut 3 hearts out of cardboard, red paper, and aluminum foil.
2. Holding the cardboard heart, glue red paper heart to one side and aluminum foil heart to the other.
3. Write a message on the paper side if desired.
4. Pierce a hole and loop a long pink ribbon through top of heart to make a necklace.

Independence Day Parade

STARS AND STRIPES CROWN

Scissors, white and blue construction paper, red yarn, paper glue or paste, pencil, silver glitter, stapler

1. Cut a band of white paper 3 inches wide and long enough to fit around child's head.
2. Cut seven pieces of yarn the length of the white band. Glue the first piece of yarn to top edge of band. Glue rest of yarn 1/2 inch apart to form the thirteen stripes of the flag.
3. Cut a 3- by 4-inch rectangle of blue paper and glue to middle of band.
4. Use a pencil to mark fifty dots on the blue rectangle: nine rows, alternating six dots and five dots per row.
5. Place a dab of glue on each pencil mark. Sprinkle glitter over glue, let dry, and shake off excess.
6. Fit crown to child's head and staple ends of band together.

PAPER FLAG

Rectangular sheet of white paper, red and blue construction paper, scissors, paper glue or paste, pencil, sliver glitter, newspaper, tape

1. Cut seven strips of red paper and glue onto white paper.
2. Cut small blue rectangle and glue to top left corner.
3. Follow steps 4 and 5 of Stars and Stripes Crown.
4. Take a large sheet of newspaper and fold in half. Start at one corner and roll tightly into a long stick shape. Tape securely.
5. Attach flag to top.

Variation: Tape red, white, and blue crepe-paper streamers to end of newspaper rolled into stick for a fireworks baton.

Leaf Rubbings

various-shaped leaves, tracing or parchment paper, crayons, scissors, tape, yarn

Collect a variety of nicely shaped leaves and place them on a flat surface. Cover each leaf with a piece of paper. Remove the paper wrapper from each of the crayons. Rub the long side of the crayon on the surface of the paper over the leaf. Repeat with different colored crayons until the image of the leaf comes through onto the paper. Cut out the leaf shapes and tape them to a long string of yarn. String the leaves in a window or along a wall. The next time the wind blows, what do the "colors of the wind" tell you?

Mouth Puppets

crayons, 8½" x 11" sheet of paper, glue

1. Fold the sheet of paper into three
   equal sections, lengthwise.

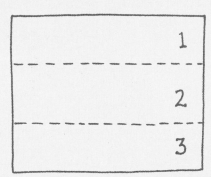

2. Then fold it in half width-wise,
   to make a tent.

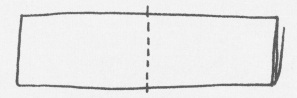

3. Fold each half of the tent in half
   again to create a W shape.

4. Draw an animal face on the outside and a mouth on the inside. You can also glue on ears, tongues, whiskers, as you like. Tuck your hand into the openings, and chatter away!

Noisemakers

PAPER WHISTLE

Fold a piece of paper in half and cut a hole at the middle of the fold. Now, fold each side back so there is a crease facing you (see right). Hold your lips against the front crease and blow to produce an ear-splitting whistle!

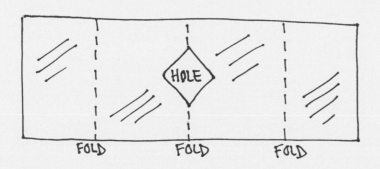

FOLD   FOLD   FOLD

HOLE

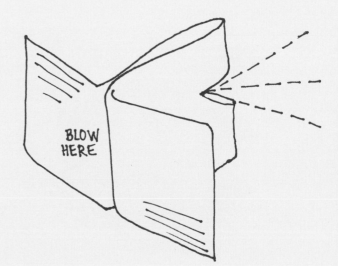

BLOW HERE

COMB WARBLER

Fold a piece of tissue paper over a medium-size hair comb. Place your lips against the comb and sing or hum to create a truly weird sound and tickling sensation.

KAZOO

Take a square of waxed paper and cover one end of an empty toilet paper roll. Secure the waxed paper with tape or a rubber band and make two slits in it. Hum through the open end of the tube to create a kazoo-like sound.

WHISTLING GRASS

Find a wide, unbroken blade of grass about as long as your finger. Hold the blade of grass between your thumbs by pressing the flat sides of the grass with the sides of your thumbs. Your other fingers should be held in loose fists, and your thumbnails should be facing you. There should be a small gap, between the first and second joints on your thumbs, where you can see the blade of grass. Make sure the grass is stretched tightly across this gap. Put your lips to the hole and blow. You should make a high piercing whistle. If you're not getting a sound, try stretching the grass tighter or finding a broader blade.

34

Animal Masks

paper plate, scissors, crayons, construction paper, glue, hole punch, yarn
optional: tissue paper, glitter, pipe cleaners

1. With the help of an adult, place a clean paper plate over your face and mark where your eyes should go. Cut out your peepholes.

2. Using crayons, start drawing the animal face onto the mask. Remember that almost all animals have a mouth, whether it's a lion's bearded scowl, or a pair of insect mandibles.

3. Draw in a nose. Add some hairs if you are a mammal, scales if you are feeling reptilian, or feathers to fluff in the birdbath. Pipe cleaners and glue make for good whiskers. Ears, jaws, and tongues can be made from construction paper, and the bottoms of egg cartons create great buggy eyes. Colored yarn also serves as a nice furry mane.

4. When you finish decorating, punch a hole on either side of the mask. String two pieces of yarn through the holes and knot them in place. To wear your mask, tie both ends together behind your head. Instant MANIMAL!

Snowy Day Fun

SNOW FAMILY
at least 4 inches of fresh snow,
sticks, buttons

1. Start by making a big snowball, and then rolling it around in the snow, changing directions every so often to make it nice and round. Keep rolling the ball in fresh snow until it's as large as you want it.
2. Make three snowballs: a large base, a medium body, a small head. Pile them on top of one another.
3. Use sticks for arms and buttons for eyes, nose, and mouth. Instead of making just one snowman, make an entire snow family modeled after your own. Dress up each snowperson with a personal belonging of each family member!

SNOW ANGELS
snow

1. Have your little angel lay on a fresh patch of snow.
2. He or she should go through the motion of "jumping jacks," but while laying on the ground.
3. Help your child get up carefully so as not to disturb the angel impression.

Starry-Night Snow Globe

Glass or plastic jar with a wide mouth and tightly fitting lid, aluminum foil, glow-in-the-dark tape (optional), glitter, distilled water, dishwashing liquid, black electrical tape

1. Wash the jar and remove any labels.
2. Mold a crescent-moon shape out of the aluminum foil. If you wish, cover it in glow-in-the-dark tape. Put the moon in the jar.
3. Sprinkle glitter into the jar until the bottom is covered.
4. Fill the jar with distilled water all the way to the top. Add a drop of dishwashing liquid to the water to make sure it doesn't get cloudy or moldy.
5. Screw the lid on tightly and wrap a piece of black electrical tape around the bottom to make sure the lid doesn't come off.
6. To have a starry night any time, turn the jar over and gently shake.

Tiny Boats

PEANUT CANOE

Cut the top off of a large peanut lengthwise, making sure to leave the ends on. Remove the peanut to hollow out the inside. Add a brave little matchstick sailor, and your peanut canoe is ready for action!

WALNUT OR EGGSHELL BOAT

Make a sail by drawing a design or picture on a small piece of paper using crayons or markers. Make two small slits at the top and bottom, and then weave a toothpick through the slits to create a mast. Use craft glue or a small piece of craft gum to attach the toothpick mast to the inside at one end of half a walnut shell for a tiny one-man sea cruiser. You could also use one half of a clean eggshell.

MATCHSTICK PEOPLE

Remove a match from a matchbook. Using a pair of scissors, cut a slit in the bottom to about halfway up and slightly separate the two pieces. Be careful not to break them. These will be the legs. Carefully make two slits on either side of the matchstick from the middle up to a little bit before the matchstick head. These will be the arms. Gently fold the legs to make your matchstick person sit in a boat.

ALUMINUM-FOIL BOAT

Start with a piece of foil approximately 6 inches square. Fold the square in half and slightly scrunch and pinch the two ends closed. Reopen the boat gently. Stand the boat on a flat surface and use your fingers to flatten the bottom down a little so it will float.

Nursery Rhymes

Baa, Baa, Black Sheep

Baa, baa, black sheep,
Have you any wool?
Yes sir, yes sir,
Three bags full;

One for my master,
One for my dame,
But none for the little boy
Who cries in the lane.

44

Curly-Locks

Curly-Locks, Curly-Locks,
wilt thou be mine?

Thou shalt not wash the dishes,
nor yet feed the swine;

But sit on a cushion,
and sew a fine seam,

And feed upon strawberries,
sugar, and cream.

Five Toes

This little pig went to market;

This little pig stayed at home;

This little pig had roast beef;

This little pig had none;

This little pig said, "Wee, wee!

I can't find my way home."

Humpty

Humpty Dumpty
sat on a wall,

Humpty Dumpty
had a great fall;

All the King's horses,
and all the King's men

Cannot put Humpty Dumpty
together again.

Dumpty

52

Jack and Jill

Jack and Jill went up the hill,
to fetch a pail of water;

Jack fell down,
and broke his crown, and
Jill came tumbling after.

Then up Jack got and
off did trot, as fast
as he could caper,

To old Dame Dob,
who patched his nob with
vinegar and brown paper.

Little Bo-Peep

Little Bo-Peep
has lost her sheep,

And can't tell
where to find them;

Leave them alone,
and they'll come home,

54

And bring
their tails behind them.

Little Miss Muffet

Little Miss Muffet
Sat on a tuffet,
Eating of curds and whey;

There came a big spider,
And sat down beside her,

And frightened
Miss Muffet away.

56

Mary's Lamb

Mary had a little lamb,
It's fleece was white as snow;
And everywhere that Mary went
The Lamb was sure to go.

He followed her to school one day;
Which was against the rule;
It made the children laugh and play
To see a lamb at school.

And so the teacher turned him out,
But still he lingered near,
And waited patiently about
Till Mary did appear.

Then he ran to her, and laid
His head upon her arm,
As if he said, "I'm not afraid,—
You'll keep me from all harm."

Old King Cole

Old King Cole was a
merry old soul, and a
merry old soul was he;

He called for his pipe,
and he called for his bowl,
and he called for his
fiddlers three!

And every fiddler, he had a fine fiddle, and a very fine fiddle had he.

"Twee tweedle dee, tweedle dee" went the fiddlers.

Oh, there's none so rare as can compare with King Cole and his fiddlers three.

Old Mother Hubbard

Old Mother Hubbard
Went to the cupboard,

To give her poor dog a bone;
But when she got there

The cupboard was bare,
And so the poor dog had none.

One, two,
Buckle my shoe;

Three, four,
Knock at the door;

Five, six,
Pick up sticks;

Seven, eight,
Lay them straight;

One, Two,
Buckle My

Shoe

Nine, ten,
A good, fat hen;

Eleven, twelve,
Dig and delve;

Thirteen, fourteen,
Maids a-courting;

Fifteen, sixteen,
Maids in the kitchen;

Seventeen, eighteen,
Maids a-waiting;

Nineteen, twenty,
My plate's empty.

One.

Two, Three

One, two, three, four, five,
Once I caught a fish alive.
Six, seven, eight, nine, ten,
But I let it go again.
Why did you let it go?
Because it bit my finger so.
Which finger did it bite?
The little one upon the right.

Pat-a-Cake

Pat-a-cake, pat-a-cake,
Baker's man!

So I do, master,
As fast as I can.

Pat it, and prick it,
And mark it with T,

Put it in the oven
For Tommy and me.

69

Rub-a-dub-dub
Three men in a tub.

The butcher, the baker
And the candlestick maker.

Dub

There Was an

There was an old woman
who lived in a shoe.

She had so many
children she didn't
know what to do.

Old Woman

She gave them
some broth
without any bread.

She kissed them all
soundly and
put them to bed.

GAMES

Balloons

 This is the way
We blow our balloon.

Blow!

Blow!

Blow!

 This is
the way
We break
our balloon.

 Oh, oh, no!

Do Your Ears Hang Low?

Do your ears
hang low?

Do they wobble
to and fro?

Can you tie
them in a knot?

Can you tie
them in a bow?

Can you throw
them over your
shoulder like a

continental
soldier?

Do your ears
hang low?

78

Head, Shoulders, Knees & Toes!

Head, shoulders, knees and toes, knees and toes!
Head, shoulders, knees and toes, knees and toes!

Eyes and ears and mouth and nose,
head, shoulders, knees and toes, knees and toes!

Five Little Monkeys

(Bounce five fingers)
Five little monkeys
jumping on the bed.

One fell off and
bumped his head.

Mama called the doctor, and
the doctor said, "That's what
you get for jumping
on the bed!"

*(Repeat for four, three, two,
one little monkey, bouncing
correct number of fingers.
End with "...no more monkeys
jumping on the bed!")*

Follow the Leader

An active and daring child should be chosen as leader. The others follow him or her, one behind the other, as closely as they can, doing as the leader does and going where the leader goes. The leader can choose to hop, skip, and jump; or crawl under and climb over obstacles. If anyone fails to accomplish any one feat, he or she leaves the line. The final person left in the line becomes the next leader.

Duck, Duck, Goose

1. Choose one player to be "It." Everyone else sits in a circle facing each other.

2. "It" walks around the outside of the circle, tapping each person on the head, calling out the word "Duck." When "It" calls a player "Goose!" that player must get up and chase "It" around the circle and tag "It".

3. If Goose does not tag "It" before "It" makes it all the way around the circle and back into Goose's spot, then Goose becomes "It" and the game starts over. If Goose does catch "It," then Goose gets to sit back in the circle and "It" starts again.

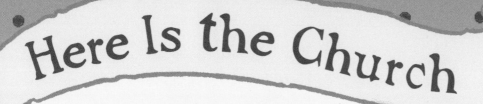

Here Is the Church

Here is the church.

Here is the steeple.

Open the doors.

And see all the people.

The Itsy-Bitsy Spider

The itsy-bitsy spider climbed up the water spout.

Down came the rain

And washed the spider out!

Out came the sun

and dried up all the rain.

And the itsy-bitsy spider went up the spout again!

Leap Frog

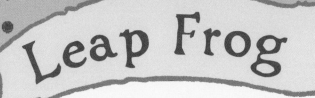

1. Everybody stands in a straight line.

2. Each player crouches in frog position by bending at the knees. Evenly distribute your weight between your hands and feet. Make sure you all have your heads down.

3. Start with the "frog" at the end of the line. She places her hands on the back of the frog in front of her, and leaps over that person with her legs on either side of him/her. She continues down the line until she's jumped over everybody. Then the new last frog begins jumping, and so on.

Open, Shut Them

Open,
Shut them.

Give a
little clap.

Open, Shut them.
Open, Shut them.

Place them
in your lap.

*(Creep hands
up, tickling)*
Creep them,
creep them.

Creep them, creep them.
Right up to your chin.

Open wide
your little mouth,
But do not let
them in.

Ring Around the Rosey

At least two players join hands, forming a ring, and walk around singing:

Ring around the rosey
A pocket full of posies
Ashes, ashes,
We all fall down.

After singing the last line, players collapse to the floor. Then they get up and begin singing all over again.

Shadow Puppets

hands, light, a wall

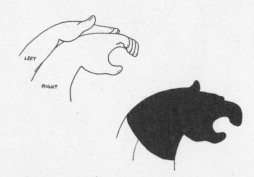

Pull your right thumb away from your fingers to make a panther roar.

Wiggle your fingers to make the spider walk.

Twitch your rabbit's ears by moving the third and fourth fingers of your left hand.

Move your right thumb for a boxing wallaby.

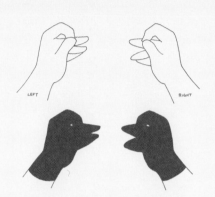

Shift your fourth
finger and pinky to
make the birds talk.

Wave your hands to
make the bird fly.

paper plate

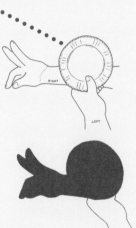

Try moving your hands so
that your dog sniffs the air.

Pull back your right
arm to make the snail
disappear into its shell.

Simon Says

One child is "Simon." The other children spread out near Simon and wait for his directions. Simon will give the group commands, like "touch toes," "rub belly," "hop on one foot," etc. If Simon precedes each command with the phrase "Simon says" the group has to follow his command. If his directions are not preceded with "Simon says," anyone who follows the command is out of the game. The last person in the game wins and is Simon in the next round. An adult can play this game with one child to test his or her concentration and focus.

Hilda Austin

The Wheels on the Bus

(*Roll fists*)
The wheels on the bus
Go round and round,
Round and round,
Round and round.
The wheels on the bus
Go round and round,
All over town!

The driver on the bus
Goes *"Move to the rear!*
Move to the rear!
Move to the rear!"
The driver on the bus
Goes *"Move to the rear!"*
All over town!

(Jump up and down)
The people on the bus
Go up and down,
Up and down,
Up and down.
The people on the bus
Go up and down,
All over town!

The babies on the bus
Go *"Wah! Wah! Wah!"*
"Wah! Wah! Wah!"
"Wah! Wah! Wah!"
The babies on the bus
Go *"Wah! Wah! Wah!"*
All over town!

The mothers on the bus
Go *"Shh, shh, shh!"*
"Shh, shh, shh!"
"Shh, shh, shh!"
The mothers on the bus
Go *"Shh, shh, shh!"*
All over town!

(Also: Wipers . . . swish;
money . . . jingle jangle;
doors . . . open and shut)

The Animal Fair

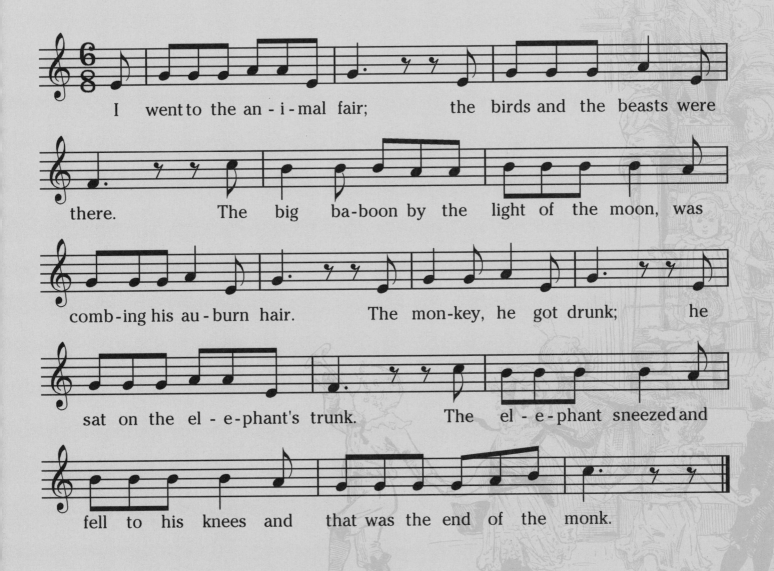

I went to the an-i-mal fair; the birds and the beasts were there. The big ba-boon by the light of the moon, was comb-ing his au-burn hair. The mon-key, he got drunk; he sat on the el-e-phant's trunk. The el-e-phant sneezed and fell to his knees and that was the end of the monk.

The ants go march - ing one by one, Hur --

rah, _____ Hur - rah, _____ The

ants go march - ing one by one, Hur --

rah, _____ Hur - rah, _____ The

ants go march - ing one by one, The

Marching

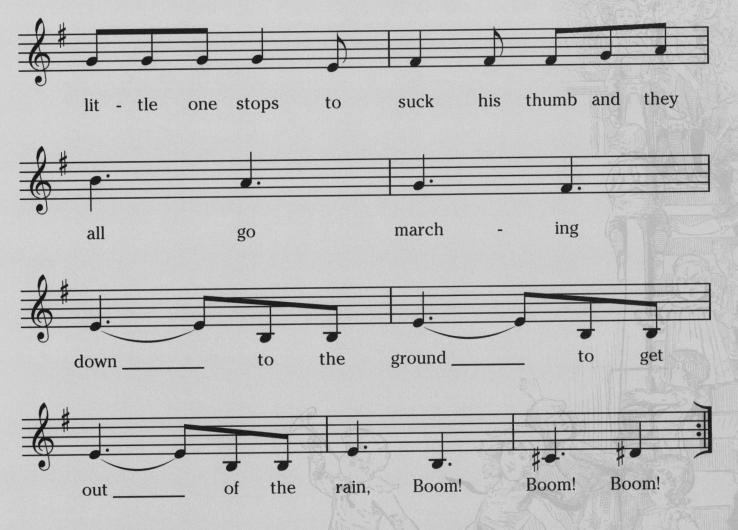

lit - tle one stops to suck his thumb and they

all go march - ing

down _____ to the ground _____ to get

out _____ of the rain, Boom! Boom! Boom!

2 ...two by two...tie his shoe...
3 ...three by three...climb a tree...
4 ...four by four...shut the door...
5 ...five by five...take a dive...
6 ...six by six...pick up sticks...

7 ...seven by seven...pray to heaven...
8 ...eight by eight...shut the gate...
9 ...nine by nine...check the time...
10 ...ten by ten...say "THE END!"

The Big Rock Candy Mountain

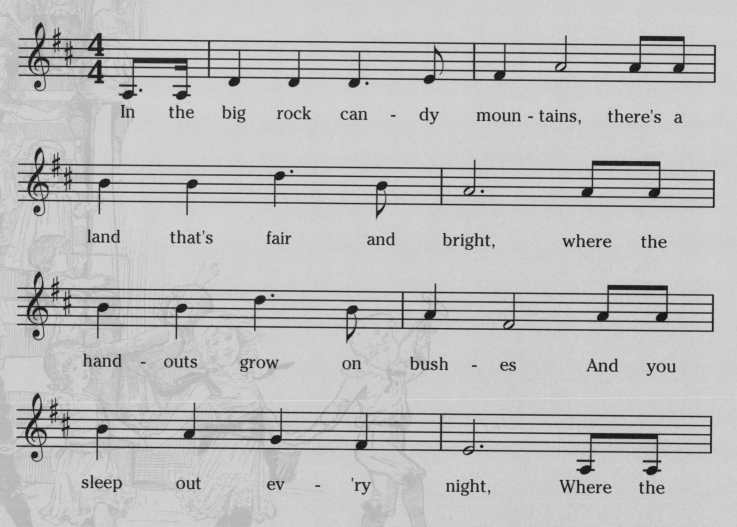

In the big rock can - dy moun - tains, there's a

land that's fair and bright, where the

hand - outs grow on bush - es And you

sleep out ev - 'ry night, Where the

The Big Rock Candy Mountain

box - cars are all emp - ty And the

sun shines ev - 'ry day, Oh, I'm

bound to go where there ain't no snow, Where the

rain don't fall and the wind don't blow, In the

big rock can - dy moun - tains.

The Big Rock Candy Mountain

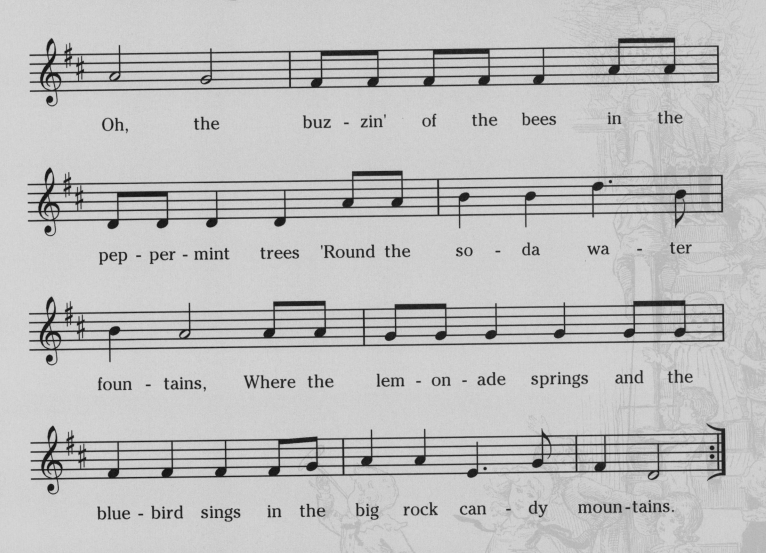

Oh, the buz - zin' of the bees in the pep - per - mint trees 'Round the so - da wa - ter foun - tains, Where the lem - on - ade springs and the blue - bird sings in the big rock can - dy moun - tains.

2. In the Big Rock Candy Mountains,
   You never change your socks,
   And little streams of lemonade
   Come a-tricklin' down the rocks,
   The hobos there are friendly

And their fires all burn bright,
There's a lake of stew and soda, too,
You can paddle all around 'em in a big canoe
In the Big Rock Candy Mountains.

Chorus

Bingo

There was a farm-er had a dog and Bin-go was his name - o.

B - I - N-G-O, B - I - N-G-O,

B - I - N-G-O, and Bin-go was his name - o.

Bingo

2. There was a farmer had a dog and Bingo was his name-o.
(Clap)-I-N-G-O, (Clap)-I-N-G-O, (Clap)-I-N-G-O,
And Bingo was his name-o.

There was a farmer had a dog and Bingo was his name-o.
(Clap)-(Clap)-N-G-O, (Clap)-(Clap)-N-G-O, (Clap)-(Clap)-N-G-O,
And Bingo was his name-o.

There was a farmer had a dog and Bingo was his name-o.
(Clap)-(Clap)-(Clap)-G-O, (Clap)-(Clap)-(Clap)-G-O, (Clap)-(Clap)-(Clap)-G-O,
And Bingo was his name-o.

There was a farmer had a dog and Bingo was his name-o.
(Clap)-(Clap)-(Clap)-(Clap)-O, (Clap)-(Clap)-(Clap)-(Clap)-O,
(Clap)-(Clap)-(Clap)-(Clap)-O,
And Bingo was his name-o.

There was a farmer had a dog and Bingo was his name-o.
(Clap)-(Clap)-(Clap)-(Clap)-(Clap), (Clap)-(Clap)-(Clap)-(Clap)-(Clap),
(Clap)-(Clap)-(Clap)-(Clap)-(Clap),

Down by the Station

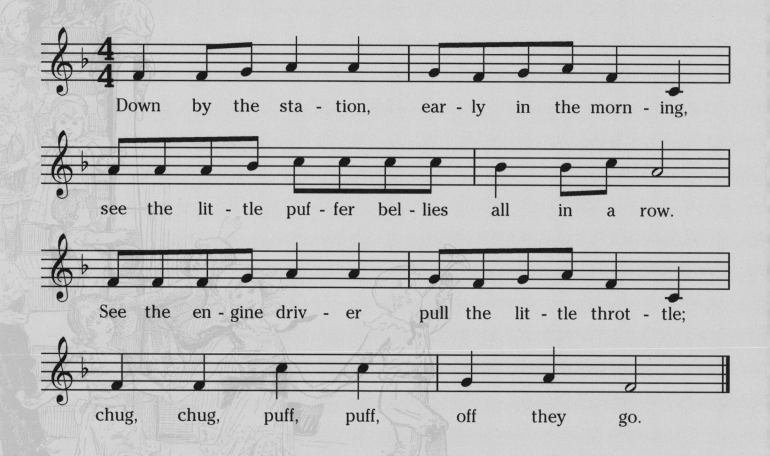

Down by the sta - tion, ear - ly in the morn - ing,

see the lit - tle puf - fer bel - lies all in a row.

See the en - gine driv - er pull the lit - tle throt - tle;

chug, chug, puff, puff, off they go.

114

The Hokey Pokey

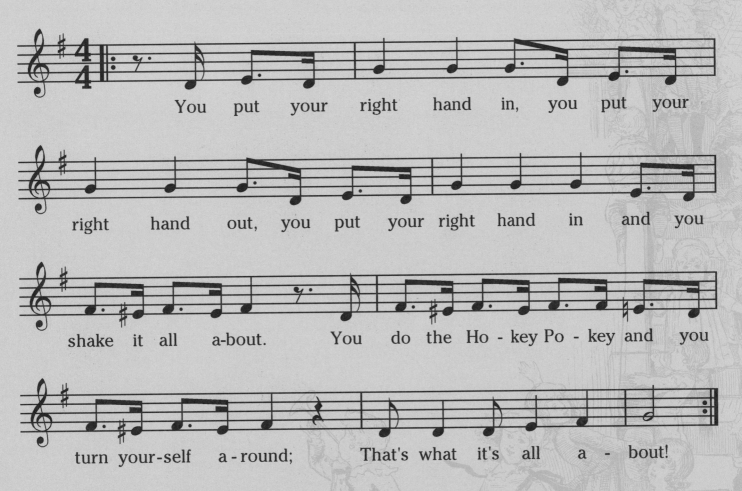

You put your right hand in, you put your right hand out, you put your right hand in and you shake it all a-bout. You do the Ho - key Po - key and you turn your-self a - round; That's what it's all a - bout!

2. You put your left hand in . . .

3. Right foot in

4. Left foot in

5. Right shoulder in

6. Left shoulder in

7. Right hip in

8. Left hip in

9. Head in

10. Whole self in

If You're Happy

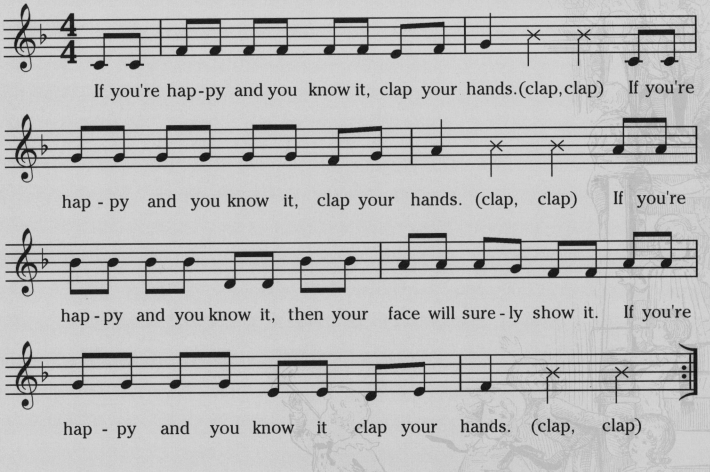

If you're hap-py and you know it, clap your hands.(clap,clap) If you're

hap - py and you know it, clap your hands. (clap, clap) If you're

hap-py and you know it, then your face will sure-ly show it. If you're

hap - py and you know it clap your hands. (clap, clap)

2. ...stomp your feet (stomp, stomp)...

3. ...shout hurray (Hurray!)...

4. ...do all three (clap, clap, stomp, stomp, hurray!)

119

Inchworm

Two and two are four, four and four

Inch - worm, inch - worm, mea - sur - ing the

are eight, Eight and eight are six - teen,

ma - ri - golds. You and your a - rith - ma - tic, you'll

six - teen and six - teen are thir - ty - two,

prob - a - bly go far. _____

2. Inch worm, Inchworm, measuring the marigolds,
seems to me you'd stop and see how beautiful they are.

Little Bunny

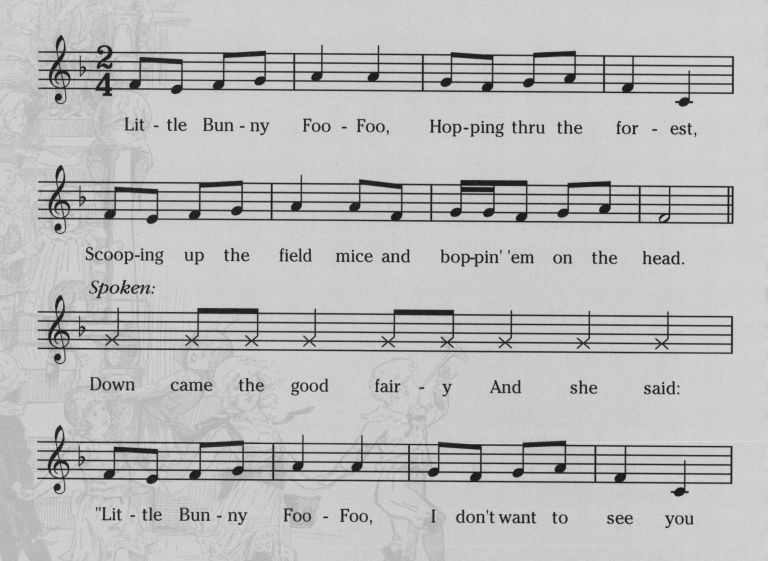

Lit - tle Bun - ny Foo - Foo, Hop-ping thru the for - est,

Scoop-ing up the field mice and bop-pin' 'em on the head.

Spoken:

Down came the good fair - y And she said:

"Lit - tle Bun - ny Foo - Foo, I don't want to see you

Foo Foo

Scoop-ing up the field mice and bop-pin' 'em on the head.

Spoken:

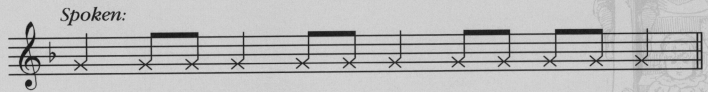

I'll give you three chan-ces, And if you don't be-have,

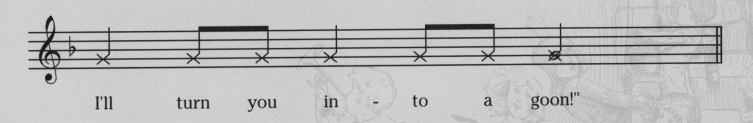

I'll turn you in-to a goon!"

Spoken: The next day:

2. Same as verse 1 except on line 6,
"I'll give you two more chances . . ."

3. "I'll give you one more chance . . ."

4. "I gave you three chances and you didn't behave. Now you're a goon! POOF!!"

Mulberry Bush

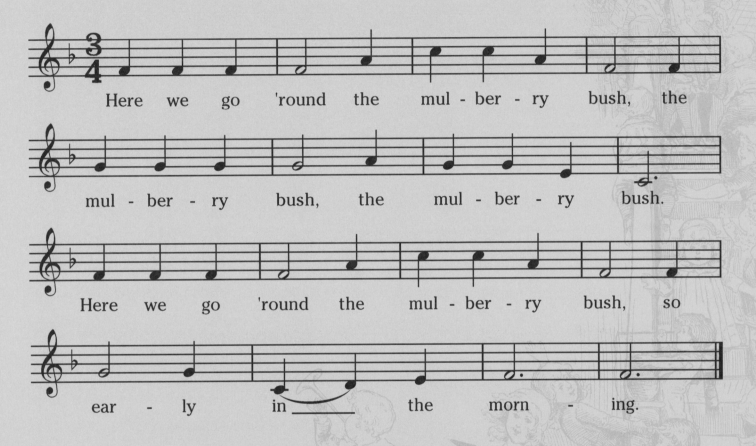

Here we go 'round the mul - ber - ry bush, the

mul - ber - ry bush, the mul - ber - ry bush.

Here we go 'round the mul - ber - ry bush, so

ear - ly in the morn - ing.

2. This is the way we wash our face, wash our face, wash our face, so early in the morning.

3. This is the way we comb our hair, comb our hair, comb our hair, so early in the morning.

4. This is the way we brush our teeth, brush our teeth, brush our teeth, so early in the morning.

5. This is the way we put on our clothes, put on our clothes, put on our clothes, so early in the morning.

Old Macdonald

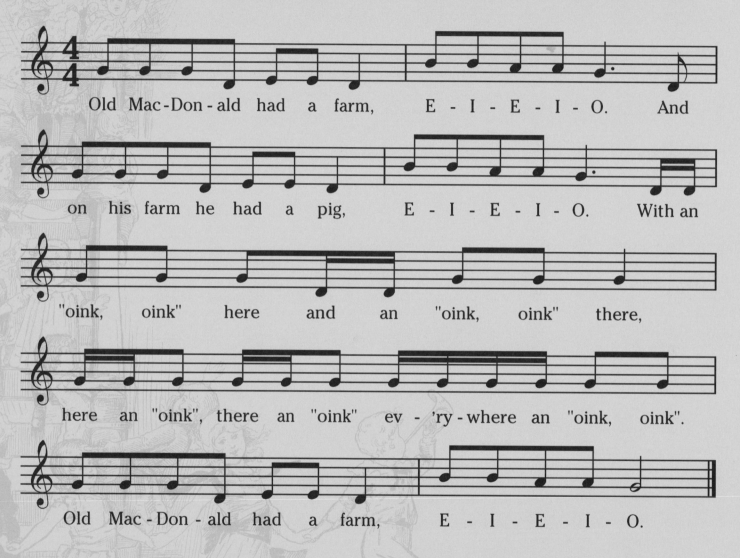

Old Mac-Don-ald had a farm, E - I - E - I - O. And

on his farm he had a pig, E - I - E - I - O. With an

"oink, oink" here and an "oink, oink" there,

here an "oink", there an "oink" ev - 'ry - where an "oink, oink".

Old Mac-Don-ald had a farm, E - I - E - I - O.

2. duck..."quack, quack"   5. cow..."moo, moo"
3. chick..."chick, chick"   6. horse..."neigh, neigh"
4. turkey..."gobble, gobble"   7. sheep..."baa, baa"

Pop! Goes the Weasel

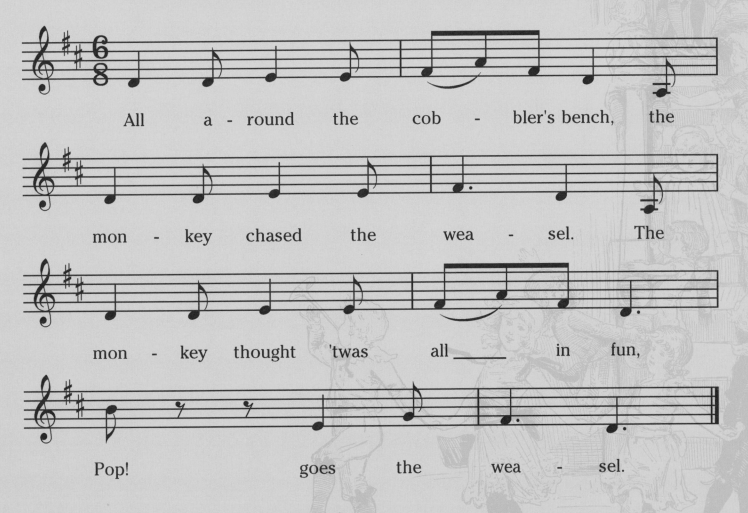

All a-round the cob-bler's bench, the

mon-key chased the wea - sel. The

mon-key thought 'twas all _____ in fun,

Pop! goes the wea - sel.

129

Rain, Rain, Go Away

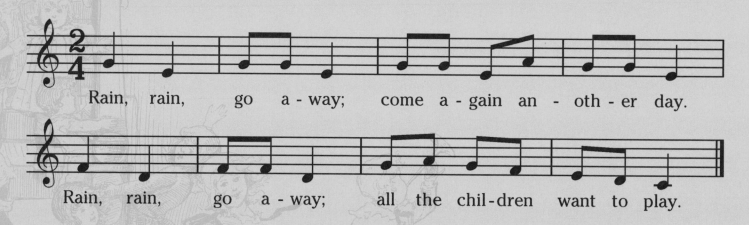

Rain, rain, go a - way; come a - gain an - oth - er day.

Rain, rain, go a - way; all the chil - dren want to play.

Shoo Fly

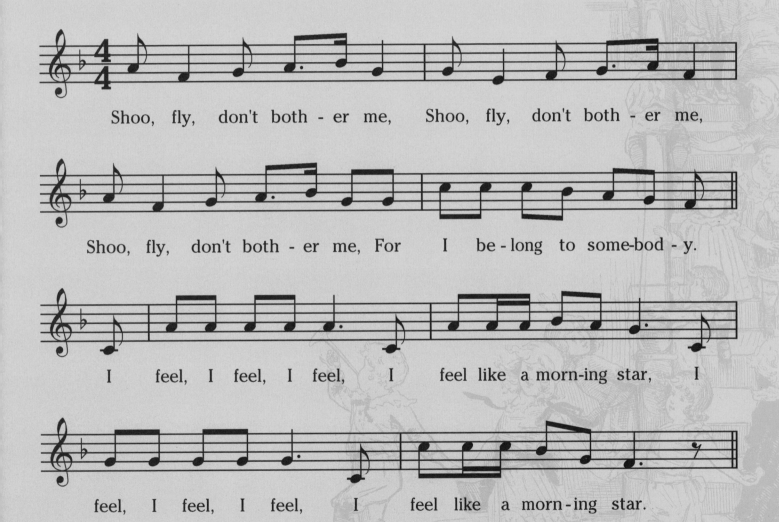

Shoo, fly, don't both - er me, Shoo, fly, don't both - er me,

Shoo, fly, don't both - er me, For I be - long to some - bod - y.

I feel, I feel, I feel, I feel like a morn - ing star, I

feel, I feel, I feel, I feel like a morn - ing star.

This Old Man

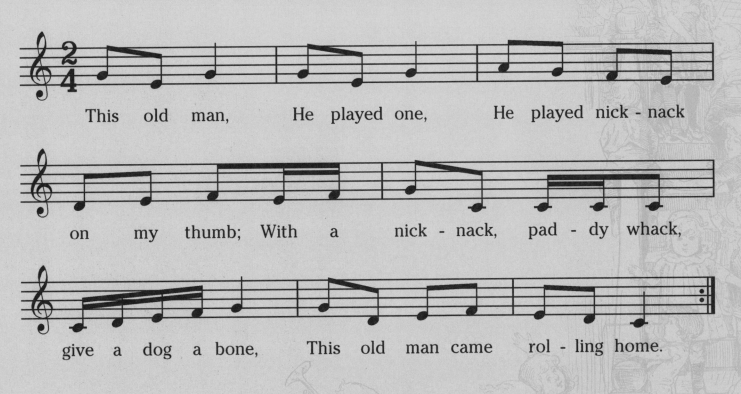

This old man, He played one, He played nick - nack

on my thumb; With a nick - nack, pad - dy whack,

give a dog a bone, This old man came rol - ling home.

2. This old man, he played two,
   He played nick-nack on my shoe;
   With a nick-nack paddy whack,
   give a dog a bone, This old man
   came rolling home.

3. . . . three . . . on my knee

4. . . . four . . . on my door

5. . . . five . . . on my hive

6. . . . six . . . on my sticks

7. . . . seven . . . up in heaven

8. . . . eight . . . on my gate

9. . . . nine . . . on my spine

10. . . . ten . . . once again

135

Twinkle, Twinkle Little Star

Twin - kle, twin - kle lit - tle star, How I won - der

what you are, Up a - bove the world so high,

Like a dia - mond in the sky, Twin - kle, twin - kle

lit - tle star, How I won - der what you are.

137

FAIRY TALES

THE BOY WHO CRIED WOLF

O nce upon a time, a shepherd boy lived in a tiny village high in the tallest mountains. Every morning, he led the villagers' sheep up a steep, grassy hill to graze.

From the shady spot where he sat, he'd often look down at the ant-size villagers and wondered what it would be like to bake bread, give haircuts, or cobble shoes for a living, surrounded by other people instead of sheep. "It wouldn't be as boring as watching sheep," he muttered. "All sheep do is eat and sleep and say *Baa* all day. I'm so, sooooo bored!" Suddenly, he had idea.

"Wolf! Wolf!" he cried loudly. "A wolf is chasing the sheep!"

The villagers immediately dropped what they were doing and hurried up the hill.

"I don't see a wolf," said the butcher, huffing and puffing from the steep climb.

"Our sheep are fine. What is going on here?" said the doctor, wiping the sweat from his brow.

"Oh! I just wanted some company!" said the shepherd boy.

"Don't cry 'wolf' when there's no wolf, or you'll be sorry," the villagers scolded the shepherd boy. But the boy

THE BOY WHO CRIED WOLF

was laughing so hard tears ran down his cheeks.

The next day, from the shady spot where he sat, he looked down at the ant-size villagers again. And again he said, "All sheep do is eat and sleep and say *Baa* all day. I'm so, sooooo bored!" So again the boy yelled, "Wolf! Wolf! A wolf is chasing the sheep!"

Again, the villagers climbed the steep hill.

"I don't see a wolf," said the butcher, huffing and puffing even more than the day before.

"He did it again!" yelled the doctor.

"Don't cry 'wolf' when there is no wolf, of you'll be sorry,"

they warned. But the shepherd boy just laughed, thrilled that he'd made his life more fun.

The next day it happened. From the top of the hill the boy saw a REAL wolf—furry, fierce, and drooling—sneaking from tree to tree, closer and closer.

"Wolf! Wolf!" the shepherd boy shouted in a panic. "WOLF! WOLF!"

The villagers heard him. But the butcher said, "He's doing it again!" And the doctor said, "I'm not running up that hill for nothing again." They thought the shepherd boy was trying to fool them like the two days before. This time they didn't come. And, just as the villagers had warned, the shepherd boy sure was sorry. With no one to help him, the shepherd boy lost all his sheep to the wolf. ☼

THE CAT AND THE FIDDLE

Perhaps you think this verse is all nonsense, and that the things it mentions could never have happened; but they did happen, as you will understand when I have explained them all to you clearly.

Little Bobby was the only son of a small farmer who lived out of town upon a country road. Bobby's mother looked after the house and Bobby's father took care of the farm, and Bobby himself, who was not very big, helped them both as much as he was able.

It was lonely upon the farm, especially when his father and mother were both busy at work, but the boy had one way to amuse himself that served to pass many an hour when he would not otherwise have known what to do. He was very fond of music, and his father one day brought him from the town a small fiddle, or violin, which he soon learned to play upon. I don't suppose he was a very fine musician, but the tunes he played pleased himself, as well as his father and mother, and Bobby's fiddle soon became his constant companion.

One day in the warm summer the farmer and his wife determined

THE CAT AND THE FIDDLE

to drive to the town to sell their butter and eggs and bring back some groceries in exchange for them, and while they were gone Bobby was to be left alone.

"We shall not be back till late in the evening," said his mother, "for the weather is too warm to drive very fast. But I have left you a dish of bread and milk for your supper, and you must be a good boy and amuse yourself with your fiddle until we return."

Bobby promised to be good and look after the house, and then his father and mother climbed into the wagon and drove away to the town.

The boy was not entirely alone, for there was the big black tabby-cat lying upon the floor in the kitchen, and the little yellow dog barking at the wagon as it drove away,

and the big moolie-cow lowing in the pasture down by the brook. Animals are often very good company, and Bobby did not feel nearly as lonely as he would had there been no living thing about the house.

Besides he had some work to do in the garden, pulling up the weeds that grew thick in the carrotbed, and when the last faint sounds of the wheels had died away he went into the garden and began his task.

The little dog went too, for dogs love to be with people and to watch what is going on; and he sat down near Bobby and cocked up his ears and wagged his tail and seemed to take a great interest in the weeding. Once in a while he would rush away to chase a butterfly or bark at a beetle that crawled through the garden, but he always came back to the boy and kept near his side.

By and by the cat, which found it lonely in the big, empty kitchen, now that Bobby's mother was gone, came

THE CAT AND THE FIDDLE

walking into the garden also, and lay down upon a path in the sunshine and lazily watched the boy at his work. The dog and the cat were good friends, having lived together so long that they did not care to fight each other. To be sure Towser, as the little dog was called, sometimes tried to tease pussy, being himself very mischievous; but when the cat put out her sharp claws and showed her teeth, Towser, like a wise little dog, quickly ran away, and so they managed to get along in a friendly manner.

By the time the carrot-bed was all weeded, the sun was sinking behind the edge of the forest and the new moon rising in the east, and now Bobby began to feel hungry and went into the house for his dish of bread and milk.

"I think I'll take my supper down to the brook," he said to himself, "and sit upon the grassy bank while I eat it. And I'll take my fiddle, too, and play upon it to pass the time until father and mother come home."

It was a good idea, for down by the brook it was cool and pleasant; so Bobby took his fiddle under his arm and carried his dish of bread and milk down to the bank that sloped to the edge of the brook. It was rather a steep bank, but Bobby sat upon the edge, and placing his fiddle beside him, leaned against a tree and began to eat his supper.

The little dog had followed at his heels, and the cat also came slowly walking after him, and as Bobby ate, they sat one on either side of him and looked earnestly into his face as if they too were hungry. So he threw some of the bread to Towser, who grabbed it eagerly and swallowed it in the twinkling of an eye. And Bobby left some of the milk in the dish for the cat, also, and she came lazily up and drank it in a dainty, sober fashion, and licked both the dish and spoon until no drop of the milk was left.

Then Bobby picked up his fiddle and tuned it and began to play some of the pretty tunes he knew. And while he

THE CAT AND THE FIDDLE

played he watched the moon rise higher and higher until it was reflected in the smooth, still water of the brook. Indeed, Bobby could not tell which was the plainest to see, the moon in the sky or the moon in the water. The little dog lay quietly on one side of him, and the cat softly purred upon the other, and even the moolie-cow was attracted by the music and wandered near until she was browsing the grass at the edge of the brook.

After a time, when Bobby had played all the tunes he knew, he laid the fiddle down beside him, near to where the cat slept, and then he lay down upon the bank and began to think.

It is very hard to think long upon a dreamy summer night without falling asleep, and very soon Bobby's eyes closed and he forgot all about the dog and the cat and the cow and the fiddle, and dreamed he was Jack the Giant Killer and was just about to slay the biggest giant in the world.

And while he dreamed, the cat sat up and yawned and stretched herself, and then began wagging her long tail from side to side and watching the moon that was reflected in the water.

But the fiddle lay just behind her, and as she moved her tail, she drew it between the strings of the fiddle, where it caught fast. Then she gave her tail a jerk and pulled the fiddle against the tree, which made a loud noise This frightened the cat greatly, and not knowing what was the matter with her tail, she started to run as fast as she could. But still the fiddle clung to her tail, and at every step it bounded along and made such a noise that she screamed with terror. And in her fright she ran straight towards the cow, which, seeing a black streak coming at her, and hearing the racket made by the fiddle, became also frightened and made such a jump to get out of the way that she jumped right across the brook, leaping over the very spot where the moon shone in the water!

Bobby had been awakened by the noise, and opened his eyes in time to see the cow

THE CAT AND THE FIDDLE

jump; and at first it seemed to him that she had actually jumped over the moon in the sky, instead of the one in the brook.

The dog was delighted at the sudden excitement caused by the cat, and ran barking and dancing along the bank, so that he presently knocked against the dish, and behold! it slid down the bank, carrying the spoon with it, and fell with a splash into the water of the brook.

As soon as Bobby recovered from his surprise he ran after the cat, which had raced to the house, and soon came to where the fiddle lay upon the ground, it having at last dropped from the cat's tail. He examined it carefully, and was glad to find it was not hurt, in spite of its rough usage. And then he had to go across the brook and drive the cow back over the little bridge, and also to roll up his sleeve and reach into the water to recover the dish and the spoon.

Then he went back to the house and lighted a lamp, and sat down to compose a new tune before his father and mother returned.

The cat had recovered from her fright and lay quietly under the stove, and Towser sat upon the floor panting, with his mouth wide open, and looking so comical that Bobby thought he was actually laughing at the whole occurrence.

And these were the words to the tune that Bobby composed that night:

Hey, diddle, diddle,
The cat and the fiddle,
The cow jumped
over the moon!
The little dog laughed
To see such sport,
And the dish ran away
with the spoon!

CHICKEN LITTLE

Once upon a time, there was a sweet, small chicken named Chicken Little. One morning as she was scratching the ground in her yard, looking for a juicy worm or two, a pebble fell off the roof of her house and hit her right on the head.

"Oh dear!" she cried. "The sky is falling! I must go and tell the king!" And with that, she set off for the palace.

A little way down the road, Chicken Little met Henny Penny, who was doing her grocery shopping. "Where are you going?" asked Henny Penny.

"I'm going to tell the king that the sky is falling! A piece of it fell and hit me on the head this very day!" Chicken Little answered.

"May I go with you?" begged Henny Penny, and Chicken Little agreed.

As they traveled down the road, they saw Cocky Locky, who was just about to go to the post office.

"Say, where are you two going in such a rush?" he asked.

"We're going to tell the king that the sky is falling!" Henny Penny said.

"How do you know it's falling?"

"Because Chicken Little told me so!" said Henny Penny with annoyance.

"A piece of it fell on my head!" declared Chicken Little.

CHICKEN LITTLE

Forgetting his letters, Cocky Locky asked, "May I go with you?"

"Certainly," Chicken Little and Henny Penny answered, and the three were off.

They had just turned a corner when they almost ran into Goosey Loosey, who had decided to go to the movies that afternoon.

"Watch where you're going!" she spluttered. "What's the matter with you three?"

Cocky Locky answered, "We have to hurry and tell the king that the sky is falling!"

"The sky is falling?" Goosey Loosey asked with wide eyes, "How do you know that?"

"Henny Penny told me," said Cocky Locky.

"Chicken Little told me," said Henny Penny.

"A piece of it fell and hit me on the head!" cried Chicken Little. "I didn't realize how serious this was!" said Goosey Loosey. "May I join you?"

"Of course!" they exclaimed.

Then Goosey Loosey followed Chicken Little, Henny Penny, and Cocky Locky down the road.

After walking for some time, they decided to take a short rest. Suddenly, Foxy Loxy slipped out from behind some rocks. All of the birds looked very tasty to him, and he asked, with a sly smile, "Where are you all off to on this fine afternoon?"

"The sky is falling and we are going to tell the king!" they answered.

"But how do you know that?" Foxy Loxy inquired.

"Cocky Locky told me," declared Goosey Loosey.

"Henny Penny told me," answered Cocky Locky.

"Chicken Little told me," provided Henny Penny.

"And a piece of it fell and almost squashed me!" finished Chicken Little. "So, now we must go and tell the king!"

CHICKEN LITTLE

"But you silly birds have been going the wrong way!" Foxy Loxy told them. "Let me show you the correct way to the palace."

"Of course!" said the birds, and they followed Foxy Loxy all the way to a dark hole in the side of a hill.

Foxy Loxy motioned them in. "Just step through here. The palace is just through this tunnel, on the other side of the hill!"

Now, luckily for the foolish birds, a sharp-eyed squirrel had seen the whole thing, and before even one could set a wing in, she called to them, "Don't go in! Don't go in! All your necks he'll wring, and you'll never see the king!"

The birds turned to run, and Foxy Loxy sprang forward and almost got ahold of Goosey Loosey. But the little squirrel threw a stone and got him— BONK!—right on the forehead.

Foxy Loxy rubbed his head. "The sky is falling!" he screamed, and dove into the hole.

Happy to escape from the wicked fox, Chicken Little, Henny Penny, Cocky Locky, and Goosey Loosey all ran as fast as they could for the palace.

Finally, they arrived at the gate and were admitted inside. They were brought before the throne of the wise king, and all at once they shouted: "The sky is falling! The sky is falling!"

"How do you know the sky is falling?" asked the king.

"Because a piece of it fell on my head," said Chicken Little.

"Come a little closer, Chicken Little," said the king. He leaned forward and plucked a pebble from the feathers on Chicken Little's head.

"Look, it wasn't the sky at all! It was just a little pebble that fell on you!" The king chuckled. "Now, you should all go home in peace. Maybe next time you won't be so quick to jump to conclusions."

So, the silly birds left the palace and started on the long walk back home, weary, but a little bit wiser. ☼

FOUR AND TWENTY BLACKBIRDS

BY FRANCES LILLIAN TAYLOR

Once there was a king who was very fond of good dinners. One day he sent for his chief cook.

"Make ready for a feast," said the king. "Let there be many dishes. And last of all set before me a new kind of food."

The cook went away in great trouble, for she could think of nothing new.

Now, the cook was a great friend to the birds. Every day she filled her pocket with grains of rye to scatter by the wayside.

A little bird heard what the king had said. He told the other birds. Very soon a blackbird came flying to the kitchen window.

"I am king of the blackbirds!" he said. "The good cook has fed me and my people. Now we will help her."

"What shall I do, O king of the blackbirds?" asked the cook.

"Get a pie platter as large as a tub," said the bird. "And make two crusts for a pie." So the dish was brought and the crusts baked.

"Place branches bearing ripe cherries in the pie," said the bird. And it was done.

FOUR AND TWENTY BLACKBIRDS

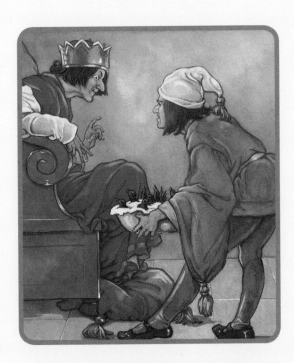

Then the king of the blackbirds called. Four and twenty blackbirds heard the call. They flew into the pie and hid among the cherry branches.

The feast was made ready. Last of all the great pie was set before the king.

"Here is a new dish, indeed," said the king as he opened the pie.

Then the twenty-four blackbirds began to sing. And their song was all about the good cook and her pocket of rye.

"Send the cook to me," said the king.

The cook came, and, behold, her pocket was full of grains of rye for the birds.

"Change every grain of rye to a silver sixpence," said the king. "And after this let the birds be fed every day."

Then the blackbirds sang a new song. All the people learned it and sang it again and again.

And it was sung into a book and it shall be sung to you.

Sing a song of sixpence,
A pocket full of rye;
Four and twenty blackbirds
Baked in a pie.
When the pie was opened
The birds began to sing;
Was not this a dainty dish
To set before a king?

GOLDILOCKS AND THE THREE BEARS

Once upon a time there was a little girl whose hair was the color of the sun. Her name was Goldilocks, and she lived in a small house with her mom and dad on the edge of a big forest.

One beautiful spring morning, Goldilocks went for a walk in the forest to pick some wildflowers. She wandered deeper and deeper into the woods looking for her mom's most favorite flowers, bright purple violets. Goldilocks searched long and hard, but couldn't find a single one! Finally, she started to get hungry and decided to go home. But she had walked so far, she discovered she was lost!

Goldilocks became very afraid and sat down on an old log and began to cry. Just then a bluebird flew by and let out a beautiful loud "tweet!" Startled, Goldilocks looked up and saw through her tear-filled eyes a little wooden cottage nestled between the forest trees. "Oh, thank goodness!" she cried. "I'm sure there's a grown-up living there who can help me get back home!" And she raced to the front

GOLDILOCKS AND THE THREE BEARS

door and banged loudly with her little fists. But nobody answered. So she walked around the house till she came to a small open window and, standing on her tippy toes, she peered inside.

This is what she saw: an empty room with a crackling fire and a long table with three steamy bowls of porridge. At the sight of the porridge, Goldilocks' stomach gave out a hungry growl. "I'll just have one or two bites while I wait for this family to come home," she thought, and climbed through the window. First she went to the largest bowl and took a heaping spoonful. "Ow!" she cried, as she put the spoon in her mouth, "this porridge is too hot!" Then she took a bite from the medium-sized bowl. "Ohhh!" she cried, "this porridge is too cold!" Finally she took a bite from the smallest bowl on the table. "Mmmm," she said, "this porridge is just right." And she ate up the whole bowl.

With a full, warm tummy, Goldilocks walked over to the glowing fire where three chairs of different sizes stood: one large, one medium, and one small. "Perhaps," she thought, "I'll have a seat here in front of the warm fire while I'm waiting." First she tried sitting in the biggest chair, but it was too high. Then she tried sitting in the middle-sized chair, but it was way too low. Finally she tried the smallest chair, and it was just right! But just as Goldilocks was curling up for a nap, the chair gave way beneath her and broke in two! Goldilocks fell to the floor and landed on her tushy with a loud THUMP! "Ouch!" she cried, and stood up, brushing herself off.

"Maybe," she thought, "there's a nice place to sleep upstairs." So she climbed the log staircase and found herself in a large cheerful room with three beds of different sizes: one big, one medium, and one small. "How lovely it is in here," she thought. "I'll just lie down for a few minutes and rest my eyes." First she tried the largest

GOLDILOCKS AND THE THREE BEARS

bed, but it was too hard. Then she tried the medium-sized bed, but it was way too soft. Finally she tried the smallest bed, and it was just right. Before she knew it, Goldilocks had fallen fast asleep.

As Goldilocks dreamed upstairs of warm porridge and a crackling fire, downstairs the owners of the house returned home from their morning walk. Who lived in this little cabin tucked away in the woods? Well, three bears of course! There was big furry Papa Bear, kind pretty Mama Bear, and little fuzzy Baby Bear.

"Let's eat," said Papa Bear, "I'm starving!" As the bears took their seats at the table, Papa Bear grumbled, "Someone's been eating my porridge!" Then Mama Bear said, "Someone's been eating my porridge, too!" And then Baby Bear cried, "Someone's been eating my porridge, and there's none left for me!"

Hungry and grumpy, Papa Bear went to sit by the fire and read the morning paper. But as soon as he sat down, he growled, "Someone's been sitting in my chair." Then Mama Bear said, "Someone's been sitting in my chair, too!" And then Baby Bear cried out, "Someone's been sitting in my chair, and they broke it in two!"

The three bears marched up the stairs to see if anything else was out of place. Papa Bear roared as he saw his bed, "Someone been sleeping in my bed!" Then Mama Bear said, "Someone's been sleeping in my bed, too!" And then Baby Bear cried, "Someone's been sleeping in my bed, and look, THERE SHE IS!!!"

Mama Bear gasped and Papa Bear let out a loud angry growl. Goldilocks woke with a terrible start. As soon as she saw the three bears towering over her she let out a piercing scream and threw herself under the covers! "Go away!" Goldilocks cried. "Go away!?" Replied Baby Bear, "But we live here!"

GOLDILOCKS AND THE THREE BEARS

Slowly Goldilocks peeked her head out and saw that this was just a nice normal family of bears. She explained to them how she had gotten lost looking for violets, and that she'd eaten their porridge because she was so hungry, and how the broken chair was just an accident. The bears understood and Baby Bear offered to show Goldilocks the way back to her house. She thanked them all, and asked if she could visit them again. "Of course," said Mama Bear, "if you don't get lost!" And they all laughed and hugged good-bye.

On their way back, Baby Bear showed Goldilocks a secret hidden patch of bright purple violets and Goldilocks picked a huge bunch for her mother. As they reached the edge of the forest, Goldilocks turned to say good-bye to Baby Bear, but he was already gone!

When Goldilocks got home, her parents swooped her up in their arms and kissed her cheeks, nose, and forehead. She had been gone more than two hours and they had been very worried! They were relieved to see her safe and sound at home, and her mother adored the violets!

Goldilocks told them all about her adventure with the bears and how she got back home. Her parents smiled and nodded, and praised Goldilocks for having such a wonderful imagination. At first Goldilocks tried to convince them that it wasn't make-believe, but after a while, she gave up. The three bears would have to be her own special secret.

Goldilocks never could find the bear's cottage again, no matter how hard she tried. But she did find her way back to that patch of violets, where she picked a bouquet for her mom every single week.

HANSEL AND GRETEL

O nce upon a time there were a brother and sister named Hansel and Gretel who lived with their father, a woodcutter, and their evil stepmother. Their log house stood nestled on a daisy covered hillside overlooking a big forest.

Hansel was one year older than his sister, and made sure to look out for Gretel whenever they were together. He even shared his portion of bread with her at mealtime, though he was weak from hunger. You see, times had been hard in their part of the land, and the woodcutter had very few customers who could afford to buy his lumber. Over time, he had sold off nearly all their valuables to raise enough money to feed his family. Finally, the day came when he had nothing left to sell.

At the dinner table one evening, Hansel and Gretel's stepmother served four cold bowls of stew and bitterly announced, "This is the very last of our food. The pantry and cupboards are bare, and there is no money to buy any more. So make this bowl last, for I have no idea when the next bowl will come." With that, she sat down and loudly slurped down her portion of

stew, which Hansel could not help but notice was twice as large as everyone else's. As Gretel licked her bowl for any meager remains, her stomach let out a long growl that was loud enough for everyone to hear.

"What kind of a man lets his poor children starve?" cried out their father,

"I am nothing but a failure who does not deserve the love of his family." Covering his face with his hands, he let out a great sob.

That night, as the woodcutter lay tossing and turning in bed, his wife whispered to him coldly, "We will all four die if something is not done quickly. There are just too many mouths to feed. Tomorrow we will take the children with us into the forest to chop wood. When it begins to get dark, we will leave them there alone and sneak home. They are far too young to find their way back out, and will surely die."

"Kill my own children!" boomed the woodcutter, "just to save myself?! Never!"

So his wife said nothing more about her plan and brought her husband a cup of tea to help him rest. The woodcutter drank it down gladly and fell into a deep, deep sleep. You see, his wife had mixed the tea with a special herb that causes anyone who swallows it to sleep for nearly a whole night and day.

Through the thin wall separating their own bedroom from their parents', Hansel and Gretel overheard their stepmother's beastly idea to abandon them. Frightened and confused, Gretel wept at the thought of starving to

death in the woods. With tear-stained cheeks she wailed to her brother, "Oh Hansel, what shall become of us?"

"Have no fear, Gretel," Hansel assured her, "I won't let anything bad happen to you." And he gently squeezed her hand.

In the middle of the night, while his parents lay sleeping, Hansel snuck outside and collected handfuls of bright shiny stones that glittered in the moonlight like sparkling gems. He stuffed his pockets full of them before slipping silently back into bed.

The next morning, Hansel and Gretel's stepmother explained that their father was ill, and could not come out to collect wood. So the three of them set out into the forest without him, and worked late into the afternoon. When the sun dipped below the horizon, their stepmother built a fire for the children and told them to rest while she went to gather some twigs. But she never returned.

HANSEL AND GRETEL

"Oh Hansel, we shall never find our way home!" cried Gretel.

"Have no fear, sister. I dropped a shiny pebble every few steps on our way here," said Hansel. "As soon as the moon rises it will reflect off the stones, making them twinkle like little stars. All we have to do is follow them, and we'll be home before dawn."

Sure enough, when the moon appeared in the sky, Hansel and Gretel followed the pebbles home. As they arrived at the door of their little house, their father rushed outside and scooped them up in his arms. "My dear children!" he cried, "I thought you were lost forever! Thank goodness you're home safe."

Then their stepmother angrily scolded, "You naughty children! You ran off and I couldn't find you! I thought you'd been eaten by wild animals!"

A week later, the cupboards were bare again, and the children's stepmother made a plan to take the them even farther into woods, where they could never find their way home. That night, she drugged the woodcutter's tea again. But Hansel and Gretel knew what to do. Hansel tried to sneak out to collect more stones, but, alas, their stepmother had locked the front door!

"Oh Hansel, what shall we do?" cried Gretel.

"Have no fear, sister. I'll think of something," assured Hansel.

The next morning, the woodcutter's wife gave each of the children half a stale roll and took them deep into the forest. Again she built them a fire as dusk set in, and again she left them, pretending to go in search of kindling. As the sky grew dark Gretel began to whimper in fear.

"Don't cry, Gretel," said Hansel, "I dropped crumbs from my bread every few steps on our way here. When the moon comes out it will reflect off the crumbs and we will follow them safely home."

HANSEL AND GRETEL

But when the moon rose over the blackened sky, there were no crumbs left to be found. The birds in the forest had flown down and gobbled them all up!

"Surely we will die out here!" cried Gretel.

Even Hansel was a little worried, but he put up a brave front, telling Gretel, "Don't say such silly things. We will sleep here tonight by the fire, and find our way home tomorrow."

The next day, the children walked and walked, but could not find their way out of the thick, dark forest. As night descended, a light rain began to fall and a chilly wind whipped through the trees. The children had eaten nothing since sharing Gretel's bread the day before, and both were starving and tired. As supper time approached, Gretel dropped to ground, clutching her stomach in hunger. "Oh, Hansel," she cried, "I can go no farther. You must leave me here and go ahead."

Just then, a roll of thunder cracked loudly in the sky and a bolt of lightning lifted the forest's veil of darkness for a brief moment. In that second, Hansel spied what looked like a little cottage not far ahead.

"Gretel, we are saved!" Hansel yelled, and he lifted her from the ground. As they neared the little house, the children saw that it was made not of wood and stone, but of gingerbread and candy! The roof was a layer of thick, white icing, and the windows were made of clear hardened sugar with shutters of chocolate. Gumballs and jellies trimmed the house, and a lovely white picket fence made of marshmallow surrounded the cottage.

The children's eyes went wide with glee. "Oh Hansel, we're in heaven!" exclaimed Gretel, as she ran to the fence and broke off a big piece. Hansel fell to his knees and dug out an m&m from the candy pathway leading to the front door.

HANSEL AND GRETEL

Just then, a high piercing voice called out from the cottage, "Nibble, nibble like a mouse. Who's that nibbling at my house?"

Hansel replied, "It's just the wind blowing to and fro, back and forth, high and low."

No sooner had the children gone back to munching on the sweets, when a little old lady with white pasty skin and long black fingernails hobbled out of the cottage. Hansel and Gretel screamed in fright and began to run away but the old woman called out in the kindest voice, "Don't be afraid,

my little friends. Come back and I'll fix you a hot delicious meal."

So Hansel and Gretel went inside the candy cottage and the old lady fed them hot apple pancakes with raisins and maple syrup. With their bellies full and warm, they snuggled into two small beds the old lady had made up, and she sang them a lullaby till they fell fast asleep.

While the children dreamt of gingerbread houses and white chocolate flowers, the old lady crept downstairs and pulled out a special cookbook from her bookshelf, titled *Child Delicacies.* She turned to a page with a recipe called "Little Boy Fricassee," and cackled with delight. You see, the old lady was really a wicked witch who only pretended to be kind to lure lost children into her home, where she could cook them up and eat them!

The next morning, the evil witch grabbed Hansel while he was still

HANSEL AND GRETEL

groggy with sleep and threw him into a large cage in her kitchen. Then she woke up Gretel with a hard shake. "Get up you lazy brat! Go cook your brother a tasty meal of fatty steak and milk. When he gets nice and plump, I'll bake him in my oven with carrots and potatoes. He'll be my most scrumptious child yet!" And she shoved the crying Gretel down the stairs.

For weeks, the wicked witch forced Gretel to feed her brother only the finest, richest foods. And every day she made Hansel stick out a finger for her to pinch, so she could see whether he was yet fat enough to eat. But the witch was nearly blind, and Hansel cleverly stuck out a little chicken bone instead. Gradually, the old witch became more and more frustrated that Hansel was still so thin. After a month, she could wait no longer. "I don't care if you feel like skin and bones, you'll make a yummy morsel anyway!"

As the witch prepared a special basting sauce for Hansel, she instructed Gretel to put the bread in the oven to bake. Gretel was small, however, and her arms were too short to push the loaf in far enough. "You'll have to climb inside a little ways. Don't worry, I'll hold your legs, so you don't slip," coaxed the witch, with such a big smile her lips nearly cracked. But Gretel knew the old woman was trying to trick her so that she could shove her in the oven and cook her, too.

"I won't fit in the opening," insisted Gretel.

"You stupid girl," the witch snorted, "even I can get in there. See?" And the witch stuck her head and arms inside the broiling oven to demonstrate.

Quickly, Gretel gave the witch a big push, stuffing her whole body into the burning fire. The witch screamed as the flames surrounded her, but Gretel quickly shut the oven door and held her ears until the witch was dead.

HANSEL AND GRETEL

Gretel then set her brother free from the cage and the two children danced and sang with joy. They filled up two suitcases with piles of jewels and gold coins they found hidden in a chest under the old witch's bed, and set off for home.

Two days later, Hansel and Gretel finally found their way back out of the forest. Their father cried tears of joy when he laid eyes on them, and held them so close to his chest they could

barely breath. The woodcutter's wife had been struck dead by a falling tree not two days after she abandoned the children, and their fathert had spent endless hours desperately searching the woods for his children.

"My beautiful son and daughter are alive and well," he wept,

as he kissed the tops of their heads, "I'll never let you out my sight again."

The two children gave their father the treasures they'd found, and he sold them for so much money he never had to work again.

So Hansel and Gretel lived happily ever after with their father on the daisy covered hillside they'd grown up on, in the little log house the woodcutter had built.

And, do you know? They never touched another sweet again!

THE LITTLE MERMAID

Once upon a time, there was a little mermaid who lived far out to sea, where the water is the darkest blue and so deep that no anchor can touch the bottom.

She wasn't just any girl with a fish tail; she was the daughter of the sea king and the granddaughter of the noble queen mother. Nevertheless this mermaid, who had so much to be thankful for—good friends, loving sisters, a wonderful father, a doting grandmother, and all the treasures you could imagine—was really quite miserable.

Ever since her grandmother had first told her stories about the great ships upon the surface of the sea, she had longed to know more about the lives of the humans: What did they look like? Were they like her? What did they do for adventure?

Her grandmother, too, had been very curious about the "upper world" in her youth. She tried her best to paint a full picture of human life for her youngest granddaughter. But the little mermaid's father thought the surface was a dangerous place, and made her promise not to go there until after her fifteenth birthday.

Well, one day she quite forgot her promise, and swam up to the sunlight.

174

THE LITTLE MERMAID

She came up close to a sailing ship. Careful not to be noticed, she spied on the people aboard. Among the passengers was a handsome prince. The little mermaid fell in love with him at first sight.

Suddenly a storm broke out, and the ship was violently tossed on the waves. The crew was forced to jump overboard, and the prince struggled to stay afloat. Without hesitation, the little mermaid swam to him and pulled him to the nearest shore, next to his castle. Wanting to make sure he was all right, she waited in the surf, out of sight. When he awoke, he saw a beautiful woman standing over him. Thinking she was the one who saved him, he smiled at her. Well, it turns out she was a princess, and the prince asked her to be his wife. They were to be married in a week.

The little mermaid was heartbroken. She swam down to her father's kingdom as fast as she could. But since she was not allowed to go to the surface, she dared not tell anyone in her family about what had happened—not even her beloved grandmother. The next day, she visited the dreadful sea witch and asked for her help. "I know what you have come for, my pretty," said the witch. "If you agree to leave your tongue behind, then I will grant your wish." The little mermaid agreed. "Well," snorted the witch, "you can't expect to win the prince's heart wearing those fins." Legs magically appeared where the little mermaid's tail had been. "I will give you three days to make him fall in love with you. If you should fail, I will melt you into foam," the sea witch cackled. "Your soul will be lost forever!" The little mermaid sped up to the surface, for she could no longer breathe as a fish.

She swam back to the shore where she had left the prince. He was walking on the beach with his dog when he spotted her. She seemed familiar to him, but he could not remember where they had met. And the little mermaid couldn't tell him that it was she who saved him from the shipwreck because she no longer had her voice. So they just smiled at each other, and he invited her to stay at his castle. As the days passed, he grew very fond of the little mermaid, but he was already engaged to the woman he thought had saved him.

When the week was through, the prince married the princess, and the little mermaid returned to the shore and waited to be turned to foam. Instead, she saw her sisters in the surf. They had all lost their hair. They had sold it to the sea witch in exchange for the little mermaid's life. Her oldest sister gave her a tiny dagger and told her she must stab the prince through the heart while he slept. Then she would regain her tail and become a mermaid again.

That night, the little mermaid went to the wedding ship where the prince and princess slept. She bent over their bed, and gave them each a tender kiss. She glanced down at the gruesome dagger she held, and threw it into the sea. Then she jumped overboard, and immediately turned to foam. It appeared that the sea witch's curse had come to pass after all, and that the little mermaid's soul was lost forever.

But a wonderful thing happened. The sun's rays warmed the foam and lifted it up to the sky. The little mermaid's loving nature and the unselfishness of her deed caused her to float into paradise. She became one of the spirits of the air who watch over all the little children of the world. If you look very carefully, you just might see her sitting on a cloud or sliding down a rainbow. ☼

THE LITTLE RED HEN

Once upon a time, in a very noisy farmyard, lived the Little Red Hen. "Cluck cluck! Cluck cluck!" she chirped every day, from sunrise to sunset, as she waddled busily about with her little chicks close behind her.

One day, the Little Red Hen found a grain of wheat. "Cluck cluck!" she exclaimed, looking around the yard. "Who wants to plant this wheat?"

"Honk honk! Not I," said the Goose. "I'm going for a swim."

"Quack quack! Not I," said the Duck. "I'm going for a walk."

"Then I'll plant it myself," said the Little Red Hen. And that's just what she did.

A few weeks later, the wheat was ready.

"Cluck cluck!" said the Little Red Hen. "Who wants to take this wheat to the mill?"

"Honk honk! Not I," said the Goose. "I'm going to talk to Sheep."

"Quack quack! Not I," said the Duck. "I'm going to play with Pig."

"Then I'll take it myself," said the Little Red Hen. And that's just what she did.

THE LITTLE RED HEN

A few days later, the wheat had been made into flour.

"Cluck cluck!" said the Little Red Hen. "Who wants to bake bread with this flour?"

"Honk honk! Not I," said the Goose. "I'm going sunbathing."

"Quack quack! Not I," said the Duck. "I'm going to take a nap."

"Then I'll do it," said the Little Red Hen. And that's just what she did.

"Who wants to eat this bread?" the Little Red Hen asked when the bread was ready.

"Honk honk! I do," said the Goose, drooling in the dirt. "I'm really hungry."

"Quack quack! I do," said the Duck, sniffing the sweet aroma. "It smells great."

"I'm sure you do, you lazy pair!" said the Little Red Hen. "But I did all the work, and I think I'll enjoy this myself with my family." Then she broke the bread into little bits and shared it with her chicks.

"Cluck cluck cluck!" It sure was delicious!

179

LITTLE RED RIDING HOOD

nce upon a time there was a lovely girl who wore her favorite red hooded cape everywhere she went, even to bed! Her nickname was Little Red Riding Hood.

One sunny summer afternoon, Little Red Riding Hood's mother sent her to take a "get well" basket of chicken soup and crackers to her grandmother who had a terrible cold. Her grandmother lived near their house, in a little cabin in the woods. Little Red Riding Hood loved her grandmother more than anyone else in the whole world, except for her mother, of course.

As she set off into the forest with her basket in hand, her mother cautioned Little Red Riding Hood sternly, "Do not stray from the path even to pick berries, and no matter what, don't talk to strangers! Make sure to call me as soon as you get there!"

Little Red Riding Hood dutifully obeyed her mother's instructions and stopped only to pick berries that lined the dirt trail. About half way to her grandmother's house she stooped to pluck one especially juicy raspberry from its vine, but in so doing she tripped on a root and fell flat on the

LITTLE RED RIDING HOOD

ground. The berries she had already collected scattered all over the path and her basket flipped over, spilling out everything inside.

"Oh, dear!" cried Little Red Riding Hood as she scrambled to pick up her things.

Just then, a big bad wolf jumped out from the trees where he had been watching Little Red Riding Hood for some time. He was waiting for her to walk farther into the woods so he could eat her up where no one would come upon them.

"Hello young lady," said the wicked wolf in his sweetest voice, "can I help you gather your berries?"

"Well," said Little Red Riding Hood, "you look like a nice wolf, but I'm not allowed to talk to strangers."

"I see," replied the Wolf, "then I won't say another word!" and he began picking up the berries in silence.

This seemed all right to Little Red Riding Hood. After all, her mother

didn't say she couldn't gather berries with a stranger. It took some time, but finally they put all her belongings back into the basket. "My, it's getting late," yawned the big bad Wolf, "it's almost my bedtime."

LITTLE RED RIDING HOOD

Little Red Riding Hood looked at her watch and saw she had been gone almost an hour. It normally took half that time to get to her grandmother's, and her mother would surely be worried if she didn't call soon. She explained her predicament to the wolf, and he offered to show her a short cut through the woods. Now her mother had told her not to stray from the path, but the wolf seemed friendly enough, and this was a special situation, after all.

So the wolf led Little Red Riding Hood to a much smaller trail and told her to follow it straight to her grandmother's. She thanked him for his kindness and waved good-bye.

But the wolf hadn't shown her a shortcut, at all. In fact, the new path would take Little Red Riding Hood twice as long as the one she had been on. You see, when the wolf understood that she was going to visit her grandmother, he decided that a grown-up would make a much better meal than a tiny girl. He tricked Little Red Riding Hood into taking the longer way so that he could sneak ahead and eat her grandmother before she got there!

The wolf arrived at the old woman's cabin in a flash, and knocked lightly. When she called out from her bed, "Who's there?" the wicked Wolf answered in his sweetest voice, "It's just me grandma, Little Red Riding Hood."

"Well come upstairs, my dear," replied her Grandmother.

So the big bad wolf went up to the old lady's room and, before she knew it, he leapt forward and swallowed her up in one huge bite. But the Wolf was still hungry and decided to wait for Little Red Riding Hood and eat her, too, for dessert. He put on her grandmother's nightgown and sleeping cap, pulled down the window shades, and crawled into the old woman's bed.

A few moments later, Little Red Riding Hood finally arrived. Finding

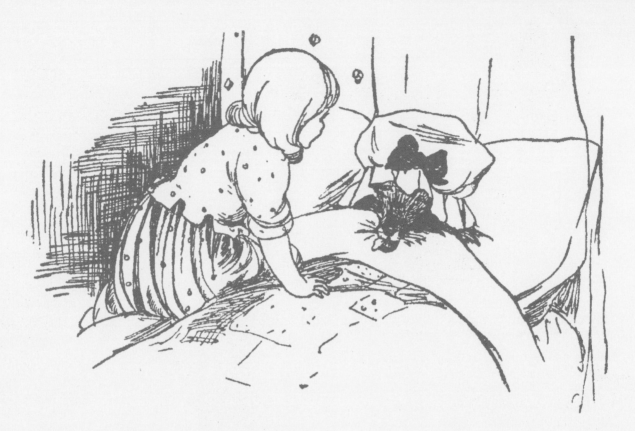

her grandmother's front door wide open, she let herself in and walked right upstairs to the bedroom.

"Granny," she said, "it's me, Little Red Riding Hood. I've brought you some soup and fresh berries to make you feel better."

"Come closer where I can see you, child," called the wolf in his kindest voice, "you know how poor my vision is." So Little Red Riding Hood took a few steps forward.

"Granny, what big eyes you have," remarked Little Red Riding Hood.

"The better to see you with, dear. Now come closer," replied the sneaky wolf.

As Little Red Riding Hood took another step she said, "Granny, what big ears you have."

"The better to hear you with," explained the wolf.

"And what a big nose you have, Granny," she observed.

LITTLE RED RIDING HOOD

"The better to smell you with. Come just a little bit closer, dear," the wolf beckoned.

Little Red Riding Hood took a couple more steps till she was standing right next to the bed. "Oh Granny, what a BIG mouth you have!" she exclaimed.

"Yes," growled the Wolf, "the better to eat you with!" And with that he grabbed Little Red Riding Hood before she could run away, and swallowed her whole in one great bite.

A hunter who had been out in the woods heard Little Red Riding Hood scream in fright and followed the sound of her voice to the old lady's cabin. He ran upstairs and discovered the wolf lounging on the bed, licking his lips in post-meal satisfaction. With his big gun the hunter took aim at the wolf and shot him once, killing him instantly. Without a moment's hesitation, the hunter sliced open the wolf's belly and pulled out Little Red Riding Hood and her grandmother, who were both still alive! Little Red Riding Hood threw her arms around the hunter's neck and thanked him for saving their lives.

After Little Red Riding Hood had called her mother to tell her she was safe, she and her Grandmother invited the hunter to stay for dinner and join them for bowl of soup and berries with cream.

Little Red Riding Hood learned a very important lesson that day about listening to her mother. And you can be very sure that she NEVER left the path or talked with a stranger EVER again (especially big bad wolf strangers)!

THE PRINCESS AND THE PEA

Once upon a time there was a handsome Prince who lived in a big stone castle with his father and mother, the King and Queen. He had everything a young man could want: wealth, good looks, and all the sweets he could eat! And yet, the Prince was very sad. He wandered around the castle halls day and night, leaving behind him a fresh trail of tear drops.

The King and Queen were very worried about their son. One evening, they begged him to explain what was wrong.

"You have everything a young man could want. What could be causing you such despair?" pleaded his mother.

"I have everything but the one thing I most long for: True love. I wish to have a princess at my side and a family of my own," said the Prince.

The King and Queen agreed it was finally time for their son to marry. But there were no princesses left in all the kingdom for their dear Prince to woo. So they decided to send him on a journey around the world, where he might find the princess of his dreams.

The Prince was gone for many days and many nights. He visited far away cities and towns, from China to Peru, and met many nice princesses. Some were beautiful, some were kind, some

THE PRINCESS AND THE PEA

were funny, and others quite serious. But none of them captured the Prince's heart. You see, there is no formula for why two people fall in love; it's one of the greatest mysteries. But the Prince felt sure he'd know when he found the right young lady.

All gloom and doom, the Prince returned home to his mother and father, who consoled him with a hundred hugs and kisses.

Some days later, a terrible storm raged across the land, shaking the walls with booming CRACKS of thunder, and charging the sky with enormous BOLTS of lightning. As the Prince lay in his bed that night, staring hopelessly out the window, he heard a banging on the castle's front door. Wrapping himself in a blanket, he descended the long winding staircase to the entry hall. BANG! BANG! BANG! The knocking grew louder and louder. As he pulled open the heavy wooden door it let out a loud CREAK. Standing there before him was a young woman soaked from head to toe and shivering from the freezing rain. As the Prince raised his eyes to meet the girl's gaze, he fell instantly head-over-heels in love.

"Come in, dear lady, come in," said the Prince and ushered her into the front parlor, where he wrapped her in his blanket and fed her hot chocolate with extra whipped cream. The King and Queen awoke and rushed down to see what all the commotion was about.Through chattering teeth, the young woman introduced herself as Princess Angeline. She had been traveling home from a trip with her chaperone when he was struck down by lightening and killed. Lost and alone, she wandered along the road, till she found herself at the walls of the castle. She thanked the King and Queen for

THE PRINCESS AND THE PEA

their hospitality and, especially, the Prince, whom she couldn't take her eyes off of.

The Queen could see her son was smitten with this beautiful girl, but how could she be certain the girl was telling the truth about being a princess? Suddenly, she thought of a way to test the girl's honesty. She called in one of her maids and instructed her to place a single pea under a pile of ten mattresses in the guest room, where Angeline was to sleep. Then the Queen showed the young lady to her bed, and bid a her a good night's rest.

Angeline had never seen such a tall bed! But she didn't wish to offend her hosts, so she climbed to the very top and tucked herself in.

That night the Prince dreamt only of the beautiful Princess. But the Princess did not dream of anything at all. In fact, she barely slept a wink the whole night long!

The next morning, as the Princess joined the royal family for breakfast, the Queen asked her politely, "My dear, did you have a pleasant rest?"

"Madame, I do not wish to sound ungrateful, but that was the most uncomfortable bed I've ever slept in! I felt as though I were lying upon a huge jagged rock, and awoke all sore and covered with bruises."

"Ah-hah!" the Queen exclaimed, as she clapped her hands together, for she knew that this girl must be a princess if she had the sensitivity to feel the pea beneath all those mattresses.

Two weeks later, the Prince asked the Princess to marry him, and she accepted. On their wedding day, the Prince presented the Princess with a special gift, a beautiful gold necklace with an unusual sparkling ball dangling from the end of the chain. You see, it was that very same pea she'd slept on, dipped in real gold, and covered with glittering diamonds!

From that day forward, the Princess never took that necklace off. And she and her Prince lived happily ever after. ✿

PUSS IN BOOTS

Once upon a time, a miller died and left his eldest son a mill, his second son a donkey, and his third son a cat.

"What a useless cat," the third son said, watching it sleep in the grass. "All it does is sleep, sleep, *sleep*! At least my brothers can earn a living with a mill and a donkey. But who ever heard of earning a living with a cat? I might as well just eat it and be full for a day!"

"No way!" the cat exclaimed, springing to its feet. "Fetch me a pair of boots and a sack, Master, and I'll see that you have great riches in no time."

The young man stared at the cat, for he had never heard it speak.

"The name is Puss," the cat said. "And I wear size six in a boot."

The young man did as he was asked and was impressed at how charming Puss looked in his shiny new boots.

Quick as a flash, Puss scampered into the woods, caught a rabbit, and stuffed it into his sack. Then he went to the palace and presented it to the king. "Sire, the Marquis of Carabas sends you this fine rabbit," he announced.

Though the king had never heard of the Marquis of Carabas (Puss had

PUSS IN BOOTS

made him up), he did love rabbit. "Please thank the Marquis," he said, handing Puss a gold coin.

Over the next few days, Puss brought the king a quail, a trout, and a pheasant. "Be sure to thank the Marquis," the king said each time, handing Puss a gold coin.

Meanwhile back at the cottage, which they had bought with two gold coins, the young man was amused. "Me? The Marquis of Carabas?" he said, chuckling. But he was grateful for the gold.

One morning, Puss heard that the king and his pretty daughter would be going out for a drive along the river. "Hurry, Master!" he cried. "Jump in the river and act like you're drowning."

By the time the king's carriage rolled toward the river, the young man was splashing and spluttering in the water.

"Help!" Puss cried, waving infront of the carriage. "The Marquis of Carabas is drowning! Thieves stole his clothes!" (Puss had really hidden them under a rock.)

Recognizing Puss, the king shouted orders to his men: "Rescue the Marquis at once! Send for some fine new clothes."

Before long, the young man was dressed in satins and silks. The king was impressed by how handsome he looked—but not as impressed as the princess. "Join us on our drive," she said shyly, making room on the seat. The young man climbed into the carriage and found the princess to be quite charming.

Puss dashed ahead and came to an orchard. "When the king asks," he said to the harvesters, "tell him this orchard belongs to the Marquis of Carabas."

"Okay," the harvesters said.

Minutes later, when the king asked who the orchard belonged to, the harvesters answered, "The Marquis of Carabas." The king raised an eyebrow.

By then, Puss was up ahead, giving orders to a group of fishermen.

"Who owns these boats?" the king called out when the carriage rolled by the dock.

PUSS IN BOOTS

"The Marquis of Carabas," answered the fishermen. The king beamed at the young man sitting next to his daughter.

Soon Puss came to an ogre's castle that was every bit as elegant as the king's palace. The ogre also owned all the surrounding land.

"Who have we here?" the ogre sneered, inspecting Puss from head to boot tip.

"The name is Puss, and I'm here to find out if the rumors are true. Can you really turn yourself into a lion?"

"Grrr!" roared the ogre, and he instantly became a ferocious lion.

"Incr-r-redible," Puss said, trembling. He was relieved when the ogre became himself again. "But I'll bet you couldn't turn yourself into a tiny mouse."

"Oh yeah?" the ogre sneered. Instantly, a tiny mouse stood in his place. Quick as a flash, Puss gobbled him up.

By the time the king's carriage arrived at the castle, Puss was standing proudly at the front gate. "Welcome, Sire, to the home of the Marquis of Carabas!"

"What a magnificent home!" the king said admiringly.

"Why thank you," said the young man, suddenly feeling like a realMarquis.

"Won't you come in?"

PUSS IN BOOTS

"Not until you agree to marry me," the princess said, blushing.

"Splendid idea!" said the king, overjoyed. "I'd be honored to have the Marquis of Carabas as my son-in-law."

"I'd be honored to marry your daughter," said the Marquis, taking the princess's hand.

They were married the next day. The Marquis's brothers, who came as guests, were amazed at their brother's success.

**"I have the cat to thank,"
the Marquis of Carabas
said, smiling proudly
at Puss. "A mill and a
donkey are nice, but
a cat in boots—now, that's
a real a treasure!"**

After the ceremony, the Marquis appointed Puss Lord of the Castle and proclaimed him the Smartest Cat in the Land. And Puss spent the rest of his days sleeping to his heart's content, without fear of being eaten by man or beast. ✸

RAPUNZEL

Once upon a time there was a couple who dreamed of having a child. Finally, their prayers were answered and they happily awaited the birth of their baby. Now, this couple lived in a house that overlooked the loveliest garden, which was surrounded by a high wall. No one dared to enter this garden, for it belonged to an evil sorceress.

One day, the woman looked down into the garden and saw a bed full of the finest rapunzel lettuce. The leaves looked so fresh and green that she longed to eat them. Day by day, as she waited for her child to be born, her craving grew until she couldn't stand it. "If I don't get some of that rapunzel, I will certainly die," she moaned to her husband.

Her husband loved her dearly and was determined to help her. At dusk, he climbed over the wall and dropped into the sorceress's garden. He quickly gathered some rapunzel and returned to his wife. It tasted so good that she desperately wanted more.

So at dusk the next day, her husband set off to fetch her more rapunzel. Over the wall he went, but when he

RAPUNZEL

reached the other side he drew back in fear. Standing before him was the evil sorceress herself. "How dare you climb into my garden and steal my lettuce?" she said, with an angry stare. "You will pay for this!"

"Oh!" he pleaded, "I beg your pardon, but I had to come. My wife saw your rapunzel from our window, and thought that she'd rather die than not have some. I came to get it to save both she and our unborn child."

The sorceress's anger quickly faded, and a smile crept across her face. "If what you say is true, then you may take as much rapunzel as you wish, on one condition: Your newborn shall be mine!"

The man had no choice but to agree, and as soon as the child was born the sorceress appeared to claim her. She named her Rapunzel, and took her away.

When the girl reached the age of twelve, the sorceress locked her in a tower in the middle of the forest. The tower had no stairs or doors, but only a small window near the very top. When the sorceress wished to get in, she stood down below and called out,

Rapunzel, Rapunzel,
Let down your hair.

Rapunzel would unpin her long, golden braids and let them fall down from the window. The sorceress used the braids to climb the sixty-foot wall of the tower. She always left before dark, and lonely Rapunzel would sing herself to sleep.

One evening, a prince was riding through the forest and happened to pass by the tower. Upon hearing Rapunzel's sweet song, he stopped and listened. The prince longed to see the woman whose voice was so delightful, but he could not find the tower door. He returned to the tower every

197

day to listen to the enchanting song. One day, the prince arrived earlier than usual and did not hear any singing; so he stretched out under the shade of a tree to wait. Soon the sorceress approached, and the prince heard her call out,

Rapunzel, Rapunzel,
Let down your hair.

Rapunzel let down her braids, and the sorceress climbed up the tower.

"So that's how it's done," said the prince. "Then I too will visit the songbird."

The following evening, the prince went to the foot of the tower and cried,

Rapunzel, Rapunzel,
Let down your hair.

As soon as she had let down her braids, the prince climbed up to her. At first Rapunzel was terribly frightened, for she had never seen a man before. But the prince spoke gently, and told her that her singing had touched his heart. Very soon Rapunzel forgot her fear, and when he asked her to marry him, she agreed at once. "Yes, I will gladly go with you, only it will take some work for me to get down out of the tower. Every night when you come, bring me a spool of silk thread. I will weave a strong ladder, and when it is finished I will climb down."

The sorceress, of course, knew nothing of their plan, until one day, Rapunzel accidentally turned to her and said, "Why are you so much heavier than my prince? It takes no time at all for him to reach me. He always reaches me in a moment."

"Oh, you wicked child!" cried the sorceress. "I thought I had hidden you safely from the world, and yet you have managed to deceive me."

In her rage, she grabbed Rapunzel's beautiful hair, wound it around her wrist, and snipped it off with a pair of scissors. The sorceress then took Rapunzel to a deserted place, and left her to die.

RAPUNZEL

That night, the sorceress fastened the braids to a hook on the tower window. The prince came and called out,

**Rapunzel, Rapunzel,
Let down your hair.**

The sorceress let down the braids, and the prince climbed up as usual. But instead of his dear Rapunzel, he found the sorceress, who screamed,

"Aha! You thought you'd find your beloved, but the pretty bird is gone from this nest, and her song is done. The cat caught the bird, and will scratch your eyes out too."

The prince was beside himself with grief, and in his despair he jumped down from the tower. He escaped with his life, but the thorns he fell into pierced his eyes. Blind and miserable, he wandered through the forest for some years, as unhappy as he could be. At last he came to the deserted place where Rapunzel was living. Suddenly the prince heard a voice that lifted his heart up. He ran toward the sound, and when he was quite close, Rapunzel recognized him. Weeping, she ran to embrace him. Two of her tears touched his eyes, and in a moment he could see as well as ever. He led her to his kingdom, where they were received and welcomed with great joy. They had a beautiful wedding and they lived happily ever after. ☼

THREE LITTLE KITTENS

BY GRACE C. FLOYD

Once upon a time there were three little Kittens, who loved to play and frisk about, and run after their own tails and each other's, and anything else that came in their way. One day their mother said, "Now children, I'm going to be very busy, so you can go out to play by yourselves, but be sure you are very good, and don't spoil your neckties nor lose your mittens." Then Mrs. Tabby washed their faces, tied their neckties afresh, put on their mittens, and sent them off. She watched them with pride till they were out of sight, then she bustled back into the kitchen and set to work to make a pie for dinner. "I'll give the children a treat," she thought, "they deserve it for they are the best children in the world and quite the prettiest, and how smart they look in their ties and mittens!" Meanwhile the Kittens were having fine games, and they rolled each other over until they

THREE LITTLE KITTENS

were quiet out of breath and sat down to rest. They were very warm too, so

> "The three little Kittens
> they took off their mittens,
> When they had done their play,
> But a Jackdaw so sly
> those six mittens did spy,
> And stole them all away."

The Kittens did not notice the Jackdaw, and presently they jumped down off the wall and ran home, quite forgetting all about their mittens. They peeped in at the kitchen door, and there they saw, O, joy! their mother making a pie, a mouse pie too, which they loved more than anything. Then they scampered off again for they knew mother did not like to be disturbed when she was busy, so they had more games until they were called in to dinner. O, how quickly they clambered up on

to their little stools, and took up their knives and forks ready to begin; the pie was baked such a lovely brown and it smelt so good! "Good children" said Mrs. Tabby, "now put you ties straight and smooth your mittens,— but where are your mittens?" Then the Kittens looked down at their paws and saw that their mittens were gone, for

> "The three little Kittens
> had lost their mittens,
> So they began to cry
> 'O, Mammy dear, we greatly fear
> That we have lost our mittens!'
> 'Lost your mittens, you naughty
> Kittens, Then you shall have no pie'"

THREE LITTLE KITTENS

said their mother in an angry voice; "Miaou, Miaou, Miaou," cried all the poor little Kits, for they were very hungry, "Miaou, Miaou, Miaou," but Mrs. Tabby was very angry indeed, and she said, "No, you shall have no pie," and she carried it all lovely, brown and steaming, away. The three little Kittens cried bitterly for some time but at last said, "Well, it's no use crying, we must try to find out mittens." So they wrote in very large letters, on big sheets of paper, that three pairs of mittens were lost and that any person who found the same, should have a fine, fat mouse as reward. Then they pasted these bills up all over the place, and ran home to hunt for their mittens again. They searched for them everywhere; they peeped in the saucepan, though, as that had been on a high shelf all day with the lid on, they could hardly have got into there, and then they felt in the pockets of their little trousers, though

they could hardly have been there either as they only wore them on Sundays, and this was Thursday, afterwards they looked on the wall where they had been sitting and where they only now remembered that they had hung them but no, they had gone and were nowhere to be found. But, at last, in the market, in the old Jackdaw's nest, they found them put out for sale, and Mr. Jackdaw close by as bold as brass, waiting for customers. Oh, how angry they were! They took old Jack, and they beat him and pulled out his feathers, and though he tried hard to peck, he was only one against three, so it was no use and at last he gave in and the Kittens took

THREE LITTLE KITTENS

their mittens and ran home with them in high glee to their mother calling out "O, Mammy dear, see here, see here, For we have found our mittens!" Mrs. Tabby was highly delighted too, and said, purring proudly and rubbing her paws,

"Put on your mittens,
you good little Kittens
And you shall have some pie,
Yes, you shall have some pie!"

So

"The three little Kittens,
they put on their mittens
And soon eat up the pie."

Although it was a very big one, but then they were so hungry and it tasted so good. They felt very happy and comfortable afterwards until they happened to glance at their mittens, and then they saw that they had dropped some gravy on them.

"O, Mammy dear, we greatly fear
That we have soiled our mittens,"

whimpered they, for they were honest little Kitties and always told mother directly they had done something naughty, and did not try to hide it.

"Soiled your mittens, you naughty Kittens!" said Mrs. Tabby, and she went and fetched her birch rod, to give them a whipping, so they all three ran off as fast as they could. But they were very sorry that they had made mother so angry, so they put their little heads together, and began to think what they could do to please her. "I know," said the eldest, "Let's wash our mittens." So they crept back to the house, very quietly, so that their mother should not hear, and they lighted the copper fire, and then they got a tub and some hot water, and soap and blue, and they took off their mittens and put them in the tub, and then they rubbed and

THREE LITTLE KITTENS

rubbed, and scrubbed and scrubbed, and boiled and rinsed them until they were quite clean. Mrs. Tabby saw, she did not say anything, but she thought to herself, "I'm sure in all the world there were never such children, they are just as clever as they are pretty." When

> " The three little Kittens had
>   washed their mittens
>   They hung them out to dry,"

The Jackdaw was perched on a bough close by. He looked such a poor miserable old thing, not at all like the sleek Mr. Jackdaw he was when he stole the three little Kittens' mittens. He said to himself "I could very easily steal those mittens again if I wanted to, but no, never again will I do such a thing, for I'd much rather have my own feathers than other people's mittens."

So the little kittens left their mittens hanging on the line to dry, and then ran indoors and said to their mother

> "O, Mammy dear, see here,
>   see here, For we have washed
>   our mittens."

Mrs. Tabby gave them each a kiss saying

> "Washed your mittens,
>   you good little Kittens—
>   But hark!—
>   I hear a mouse close by,
>   To catch him let us try."

So they all scampered after the mouse, and they caught him, and a fine fat mouse he was too. ☼

THE THREE LITTLE PIGS

Once upon a time there were three little pigs. Every week, mama pig gave each of the little pigs a quarter to do with as he pleased. And every week she counseled, "*Oink oink*! Put this quarter somewhere safe *oink oink*! and save it for something very important. You never know when you'll really need it *oink oink*!"

One day, shortly after the youngest pig turned eighteen, mama pig sat her sons down and said, "*Oink oink*! My dearest little pigs, you're not so very little anymore! *Oink oink*! Now that you are all grown up, it's time for you to go out into the world and make your fortune."

"But mama!" cried the youngest pig, "where shall we live?!"

"Well," replied mama pig, "you can take the money that you've saved and build yourself a little house."

"But I have almost no money left!," squealed the youngest pig, "I spent it

THE THREE LITTLE PIGS

all on yummy delicious candy!" —for he had run straight to the candy store every time he got his quarter.

"And I spent all mine on pretty new clothes!" chimed in the middle pig—for he had insisted on wearing the most stylish outfits.

"I'm afraid *Oink oink*! I have no more money to give to you," said mama

pig. "You'll have to get a job *oink oink*! and save up your wages."

Now, all this time, the oldest pig was very quiet. For he had saved his quarters every week just as his mama had advised, and had a nice sum of money tucked away in his piggy bank.

The three little pigs promised their mama they'd write, and off they went to seek their fortunes.

The youngest pig scraped together just enough money to build a small house made of hay and spent his days sleeping and stuffing himself with apples.

The middle pig could only afford to build a medium-sized house made of twigs and had just enough change left over to buy a sewing machine. He spent his days rolling in the mud and making himself new clothes.

The oldest pig had saved so much money, he built himself a beautiful mansion made of bricks. Every day he

THE THREE LITTLE PIGS

worked from dawn till dusk plowing and planting the fields around his house, until he was a very successful farmer.

One day, while the youngest pig was taking a nap, a big bad wolf came out of the woods and banged loudly on his door.

"Little pig, little pig, let me in!" growled the wolf as he licked his lips.

"Not by the hair on my chinny chin chin!" cried the little pig.

"Then I'll huff and I'll puff and I'll blow your house in!" barked the wolf.

"Go ahead and try!" called back the little pig.

So the wolf huffed and he puffed and he blew the straw house into a million pieces. The little pig screamed, "Oh no!" and ran next door to his middle brother's house.

"Help me!" squealed the youngest pig, "a big bad wolf is trying to eat me up and he's headed this way."

Sure enough, the wolf came knocking on the twig house door.

"Little pigs, little pigs, let me in!" growled the wolf.

"Not by the hair on our chinny chin chins!" cried out the two little pigs.

"Then I'll huff and I'll puff and I'll blow your house in!" barked the wolf.

"Go ahead and try!" called back the little pigs.

So the wolf huffed and he puffed and he blew the twig house into a million pieces. The little pigs screamed, "Oh no!" and ran next door to their oldest brother's house.

THE THREE LITTLE PIGS

"Help us! Help us!" they cried, "a big bad wolf is trying to eat us up and he's headed this way."

"Have no fear," said the oldest pig, "you'll be safe here."

Not a moment later there was a knocking on the brick house door.

"Little pigs, little pigs, let me in!" growled the wolf.

"Not by the hair on our chinny chin chins!" cried out the three little pigs.

"Then I'll huff and I'll puff and I'll blow your house in!" barked the wolf.

"Go ahead and try!" called back the oldest pig.

So the wolf huffed and he puffed, but no matter how hard he tried he couldn't blow down the big brick house.

Just then the wolf spied the chimney on the roof and thought to himself, "I'll just climb through that chimney and take those little piggies by surprise."

"Oh little pigs," said the wolf in his sweetest voice, "I'm just putting my legs in you're chimney. No need to be afraid."

"Go right ahead," said the youngest pig.

"Now I'm just putting my arms in the chimney," said the wolf.

"That's fine with us," chirped the middle pig.

"And I think I'll just poke my head in, too," said the wolf, who thought he was being very sly.

"Be our guest," called out the oldest pig.

Suddenly, the big bad wolf slid down the chimney into the little pig's house. But the surprise was on him. The three little pigs had lit a great fire in the fireplace and the wolf landed SPLAT! right in the middle of it.

THE THREE LITTLE PIGS

"OOOHHHH! OOOOOOHH! OOOOOOOH!" howled the wolf as he leapt back out of the chimney in one big jump and went running into the forest with his tail on fire!

The three little pigs shouted out with joy, and sang:

"Who's afraid of the big bad wolf, the big bad wolf, the big bad wolf? Who's afraid of the big bad wolf, tra la la la la!"

The oldest pig had so much extra room in his house that he invited his brothers to come live with him. They all went to work together, tending his farm, and lived happily ever after.

So now we see that it is better save our pennies for something really important than to spend them on silly things! ☼

THE UGLY DUCKLING

Once upon a time there was a mother duck who lived in the tall grass on the edge of a great pond. It was springtime and she was preparing a nest for her new little eggs to hatch in. One day, as she was coming home from gathering leaves to make beds for her soon-to-be ducklings, she came across a lone egg at the foot of her nest. "Oh dear," said Mother Duck, "one of my many babies must have fallen from my nest." Although the egg looked unfamiliar to her, she figured its shape must have changed during its fall, and she picked it up in her mouth and gently placed it back with the rest of her little eggs.

The next day, the eggs began to tremble and shake and, before long, cute duckling heads started popping out of their shells. Raoul was first, and with his sharp beak and narrow eyes, Mother Duck was sure he would be the heartbreaker of the great pond. Then came Uma and Prudence with their thick yellow hair. Mother Duck knew at once they would be the envy of all their duckling girlfriends. Next came Baxter and Max who busted out of their shells with such force that Mother

THE UGLY DUCKLING

Duck worried they would become the bullies of the pond.

The last egg to crack was the one that Mother Duck was the most concerned about. This was the odd little egg that just didn't seem to fit in with the others. When the head of her sixth duckling, Nathan, poked out of his shell, Mother Duck gasped in disbelief. He acted like a duck, he smelled like a duck, he even quacked like a duck, but there was definitely something strange about his appearance. In fact, this was the ugliest little duckling she had ever seen! And although she loved Nathan every bit as much as her other babies, she began to worry about what would become of him in the future.

All that spring, Mother Duck taught her six little ducklings how to paddle around, dunk for delicious insects and crumbs, and build cozy nests. Although Nathan's brothers and sisters let him play with them, the other ducklings on the great pond were not so friendly. When Mother Duck took her children for a swim, they would paddle around Nathan calling out nasty names and laughing at him. "You're uglier than a fat toad," they would sneer while splashing wildly. Though his brothers, Baxter and Max, would chase all the mean ducks away, he could see in their eyes that even they were ashamed of him.

As summer approached, the name calling and teasing got worse, and it began to affect Mother Duck's happy feathered family. Uma and Prudence, in an effort not to be associated with their ugly duckling brother, began hanging out late with other ducks and only spent time with their family when Mother Duck would put her webfoot down. Raoul whined that the stress of his home life was giving him frizzy fur, and Max and Baxter began to gain reputations as hooligans around the great pond. Nathan could see his mother's worry and decided enough

THE UGLY DUCKLING

was enough. "I'm the cause of all this trouble," thought Nathan, "I'm so hideous looking it's breaking up my family." So Nathan decided to sneak away to go live on the other side of the great pond, and hide away where no one would see him and laugh.

All through the long hot summer Nathan hid in the pond's tall grass far way from his brothers and sisters. He didn't see anyone the whole time, not even a tadpole. Then, one fall day, as he paddled on his back looking up at the clouds, he heard a voice behind him say, "Hey handsome, what are you doing?"

Startled, Nathan turned around to find the most beautiful swan he had ever seen. "Are you talking to me?" asked Nathan.

"Sure I am, handsome," she said back, "my name is Sofia, what's yours?"

"My name is Nathan, but I am not handsome."

"Sure you are, sweetie, you're just about the cutest boy swan I've ever laid eyes on," replied Sofia with a smile.

"What are you talking about? I'm not a swan, I'm an ugly duck!"

"You really don't know you are a swan, honey? Swim out with me to the still water and look down at your reflection."

Sure enough, when Nathan swam out into the open pond and looked down into the calm water, he saw that over the summer he had developed into a striking swan. Nathan was overjoyed and took Sofia back to meet his family who were all happy to see him and amazed at his transformation. Mother Duck hugged Nathan close and said that whether he was a swan or a duck, she'd always love him as her son, and made him promise he'd never disappear again. Even Raoul was impressed with Nathan's fine feathers and thick white coat.

The next spring, Nathan and Sofia got married and lived happily ever after. They even had their own litter of "ugly ducklings" who all, in their own time, emerged as lovely swans. ⚙

Index

The world is so full of a number of things
I'm sure we should all be as happy as kings.

–Robert Louis Stevenson